Selected Yiddish Plays: Vol. I

Selected Yiddish Plays: Vol. I

Works by Sholem Aleichem, Sholem Asch, I.D. Berkowitz and Peretz Hirshbein

Edited by Ellen Perecman

iUniverse, Inc.
New York Lincoln Shanghai

Selected Yiddish Plays: Vol. I

Works by Sholem Aleichem, Sholem Asch, I.D. Berkowitz and Peretz Hirshbein

iUniverse books may be ordered through booksellers or by contacting:

iUniverse
2021 Pine Lake Road, Suite 100
Lincoln, NE 68512
www.iuniverse.com
1-800-Authors (1-800-288-4677)

ISBN: 978-0-595-47142-3 (pbk)

ISBN: 978-0-595-91423-4 (ebk)

Printed in the United States of America

To the souls of all those who lived Yiddish too briefly.

Gevalt Yidn, zayt zikh niyt meyayish!

Contents

Acknowledgements

This book is the product of many minds and many hearts without which it could never have been realized. I'd like to express my deepest gratitude to Mark Altman, Clay McLeod Chapman, Dovid Katz, Reuven Avital, Yael Friedman, and Frances Greenberg. I would also like to express my sincere appreciation for the support provided by Frank Hentschker of the Martin E. Segal Theater Center, The Graduate School and University Center, The City University of New York, and Frances Degen Horowitz of The Center for Jewish Studies, The Graduate School and University Center, The City University of New York. Most of all, I'd like to thank my own fearless *tate*, A. Gershon Perecman, and my son, Adam P. Frankel, for assisting with the translations and adaptations, respectively, for believing in *New Worlds Theatre Project*, and for the infinite wisdom each of them continues to share with me. Of course, any errors are mine and mine alone.

Introduction

New Worlds Theatre Project was founded in 2005 to explore and preserve the rich vein of Yiddish dramatic literature that examines the complexity of a traditional society coping with modernization, indeed, with problems still common in 21st century multicultural societies. Our mission is to foster an appreciation among theatre artists and audiences for the extent to which Yiddish plays—and the Yiddish literary legacy—have enriched the broader landscape of theatre. In an effort to accomplish that mission, we at *New Worlds Theatre Project* translate Yiddish plays into English, adapt them for contemporary audiences, and present them in innovative productions featuring the work of creative and talented teams of theatre professionals.

Since May 2005, *New Worlds Theatre Project* has produced five of the six plays in this volume in New York City. In June 2005, we presented a full production of Peretz Hershbein's 'Carcass (*Neveyle)*' at the Common Basis Theatre, followed by a staged reading of 'Moshke *Khazer* or Under the Cross (*Untern Tzeylm)*' by I.D. Berkowitz, also at the Common Basis Theatre, and 'Dammerung or Twilight (*Tzvishn Tog un Nakht*)' by Peretz Hirshbein in November 2005 at the 78th Street Theatre Lab. In April/May 2006, the 78th Street Theatre Lab was once again the venue for our full production of 'The Amulet [Yiddish title is 'On the other side of the River *(Af Yenem Zayt Taykh)*]', the final play in our exposition of Peretz Hirshbein's experimental period. We presented 'With the Current (*Mitn Shtrom)*' by Sholem Asch in a staged reading at The Jewish Museum in December 2007. We have not yet presented our translation/adaptation of '*Mentshn* (People/Servants)' by Sholem Aleichem, but I have included it here to represent a second instance of the social conscience of the Yiddish canon.

The plays in this volume were written between 1904 and 1907, with the exception of 'Moshke *Khazer* or Under the Cross'', which followed almost two decades later. (The date for 'Carcass' is actually in question; it has been placed as early as 1906 and as late as 1924.) It was a fertile period in the world of theatre and in the world at large.

Sholem Asch

When Sholem Asch wrote 'With the Current' in 1904, Anton Chekhov's 'The Cherry Orchard' was premiering at the Moscow Art Theatre; J.M. Barrie's 'Peter Pan' was opening in London; and Arthur Schnitzler's 'The Lonely Way' was having its first production in Vienna. It was also the year Sigmund Freud founded psychoanalysis and New Yorkers began riding the subway. In 'With the Current', Asch presents us with a portrait of a young Talmud scholar who finds he can no longer resist the world awaiting him beyond the insular Jewish community he has always known. It is useful to note the context of Asch's decision that his protagonist would be a scholar. For, as Ruth Wisse writes, the scholar represented the epitome of masculinity in Jewish circles of the late 19th and early 20th century.

Sholem Asch, a novelist and essayist, in addition to being a playwright, was born in Kutno, Poland on 1 January 1880 and died in London on 10 July 1957. Asch, the son of a cattle-dealer and innkeeper, received a traditional Jewish education as a child and then moved to the town of Wloclawek where he supported himself as a letter writer for illiterate Jews in the area while seeking a secular education. Asch left Poland for Palestine in 1908 and came to the U.S. two years later. Though he subsequently returned to Europe, living first in Poland, then in France and Palestine, he settled again in the U.S. in 1938 and then spent his final years in Israel.

Asch is described as the first author to liberate Yiddish literature from the narrow confines of the *shtetl* by connecting the Yiddish world to the mainstream of European and American culture. He became the first Yiddish author to have a truly international following. In 1907, he wrote 'God of Vengeance (*Got fun Nekomeh)'*. This play, which takes place in a brothel and portrays a lesbian relationship, had by 1923 been translated into German, Russian, Polish, Hebrew, Italian, Czech and Norwegian. But New York was apparently not ready to see it in English. At the Broadway premier of 'God of Vengence' in 1923, the entire cast was arrested on obscenity charges, for which they were ultimately successfully prosecuted. Asch's other plays include: 'With the Current (*Mitn Shtrom)'*, 1904; 'Mary', 1917; 'The Way to Oneself *(Der Veg tsu Zikh)*', 1917; 'Motke the Thief (*Motke Ganev)*', 1917; and 'Uncle Moses *(Onkl Mozes)*', 1918. Asch also published twenty-four novels and two collections of short stories. In 1920, a committee headed by J. L. Magnes in New York published Asch's collected works in twelve volumes, with an introduction by S. Niger. In 1932, he was awarded the

Polish Republic's 'Polonia Restituta' decoration and elected honorary president of the Yiddish PEN Club. After writing several novels about early Christianity between 1939 and1949 (The Nazarene, The Apostle, and Mary) that were enthusiastically received in translation by the English-language press, he became the subject of serious controversy in the Jewish press. He was openly attacked in the Yiddish daily *Forward*, to which he had been a regular contributor, for encouraging heresy and conversion by preaching Christianity. Only The Nazarene (*Der Man fun Netzeres*) was ever published in the original Yiddish. The resulting estrangement between Asch and the Yiddish reading public never healed. Asch wrote his last book, The Prophet, in 1955.

Peretz Hirshbein

In 1906, a year after George Bernard Shaw's 'Major Barbara' opened in London and his 'Mrs.Warren's Profession' caused an uproar over its "indecency" in New York, Alva Fisher invented the washing machine and Peretz Hirshbein wrote the three plays in this volume. Each of the plays reflects Hirshbein's focus on mood over plot, for which he became known as "the Yiddish Maeterlinck".

Peretz Hirshbein was born to a miller on 7 November 1880 in Grodno (Melnik), Russia and died on 16 August 1948 in Los Angeles, California. Following the lifting of a twenty-one year old ban on Yiddish theatrical performances in Russia in 1904, Hirshbein was instrumental in reviving Yiddish theater. From 1908-1910, the theatre company he founded in Odessa, Ukraine performed his plays, as well as those of Sholem Aleichem, Sholem Asch, Jacob Gordin and David Pinski, across Imperial Russia. The company's high literary standards and high standards of ensemble acting had an important influence on the theatre community in the region and laid much of the groundwork for the Yiddish 'Art Theatre' movement that began shortly after the end of World War I. After the financial demise of his theatre troupe, Hirshbein traveled extensively in Europe. In 1912 he went to New York and tried to make a living as a farmer in the Catskills. After a brief return to Russia, he made another attempt at farming in a Jewish agricultural colony in Argentina before returning to New York at the onset of World War I.

The simplicity and modesty of a 1918 production of Hirshbein's '*A Farvorfen Vinkel* (A Neglected Nook or A Hidden Corner)' made theatrical history in New York where bravura was customary on the Yiddish stage. Together with fellow playwrights David Pinski and H. Leivick, he created *Unzer Teater* (Our Theater) in the Bronx in 1925, considered one of the more innovative and noteworthy

Yiddish theaters of the period. Still, the theater folded after one season due to financial difficulties.

Hirshbein's Yiddish plays include: 'The Amulet (Yiddish title: 'On the Other Side of the River [*Af Yenem Zeit Taykh]*'), 1906; 'Between Day and Night or Dammerung (*Tzvishen Tog Un Nacht oder Dammerung)*', 1906; 'Carcass (*Neveyle*)', 1906–1924; 'Earth (*Diy Erd*)', 1907; 'The Vow or The Contract (*Tkias Kaf*)', 1907; 'Parting of the Ways (*Oifn Shaidveg*)', 1907; 'The Golden Chain (*Diy Goldene Keyt)*', 1908; 'The Haunted Inn (Diy Puste Kretshme)', 1912; 'A Neglected Nook or A Hidden Corner (*A Farvorfen Vinkel*)', 1912; 'Green Fields (*Griyne Felder*)', 1916; and 'The Smith's Daughters (*Dem Schmids Tekhter)*', 1918 or earlier. Hirshbein also wrote plays in Hebrew (*Miriam* [Downhill], 1905) and in English ('Where Life Ends'; 'Joel'; 'The Last One'; 'The Infamous'; 'A Lima Bean'), as well as a Yiddish novel (*Roite Felder* [Red Fields], 1935) and an English screenplay ('Hitler's Madman', 1943, directed by Douglas Sirk).

Sholem Aleichem

When Sholem Aleichem was writing '*Mentshn* (People/Servants)' in 1907, August Strindberg was publishing 'The Ghost Sonata' in Stockholm; the premier of John Millington Synge's 'Playboy of the Western World' was sparking riots in Dublin; Florenz Ziegfeld was introducing his girls at the 'Ziegfield Follies'; and Albert Einstein was declaring that $E = mc^2$.

Sholem Aleichem, the pen name of Sholem Rabinovitch, left Russia after the pogroms of 1905 and settled with his family in Geneva. Though he adapted some of his stories for the stage, most notably '*Tevye der Milkhiker* (Tevye the Milkman)'—which became 'Fiddler on the Roof'—, Sholem Aleichem's prolific writing career included only three works written as plays: '*Mentshn*' (the Yiddish word for both 'People' and 'Servants) in 1907; 'The Golddiggers (*Diy Goldgreber*)', 1908; and 'The Jackpot (*Dos Greyse Gevins*)', 1916. It is ironic that Sholem Aleichem could not find anyone to produce his stage adaptation of '*Tevye*', a literary character Ruth Wisse considers the first Jewish hero in literature.

By the time Sholem Aleichem arrived in 1907, New York had a thriving Yiddish Theater. Both of the plays he wrote specifically for the Yiddish theater in New York—'Jewish Daughters (*Yidishe Tekhter*) or Stempenyu' and 'The Scum (*Der Oysvurf*) or Shmuel Paternak'—failed when they opened. He was willing to accommodate the needs of commercial theatre but refused to degrade the artistic level of the play, which he found much degraded in Yiddish Theatre in New

York, where in the first few decades of the 20th century, Yiddish theatre was a business and not exactly an artistic enterprise. He moved back to Geneva temporarily, giving lectures throughout eastern Europe. In 1914 he returned to New York to write 'The Jackpot (*Dos Greyse Gevins*)', whose motif of 'winning big' may have had its roots in a question raised by '*Mentshn*', namely, whether Fanitchke's new found prosperity is a good or an evil. Sholem Aleichem died in New York on 13 May 1916, eight years after contracting tuberculosis.

Isaac Dov Berkowitz

By the time I.D. Berkowitz wrote Moshke *Khazer* in 1923, Eugene O'Neill had written 'The Hairy Ape' and his first full-length play, 'Beyond the Horizon', had been produced on Broadway; Luigi Pirandello had written 'Six Characters in Search of an Author'; and Harold Brighouse's 'Hobson's Choice' had premiered in London. It was the year Adolf Hitler's "Beer Hall Putsch" failed in Munich and George Gershwin wrote 'Rhapsody in Blue'.

Berkowitz, best known as the adaptor, translator and son-in law of Sholem Aleichem, was born in 1885 in Slutsk, Russia (now Belarus). His literary career began when his 'On the Eve of Yom Kippur (*Bi Erev Yom Kipper*)' appeared in a Warsaw publication, *The Scout*, in 1903. Berkowitz published his first collection of stories after moving to Vilna in 1910, and at the same time began to translate Sholom Aleichem's writings from Yiddish into Hebrew. He also translated Leo Tolstoy's *Childhood* from Russian into Hebrew. Berkowitz emigrated to the United States on the eve of the First World War, and in 1916 founded and became editor of *Flagpole*. Four years later, he became the editor of *Shelter*. In 1928, Berkowitz emigrated to Palestine, where he co-edited *Weights* with Fishel Lachower and adapted several of Sholom Aleichem's plays for the Habima Theatre. He died in 1967.

* * * *

Like other modern tragedies that began to emerge in northern Europe in the 19th century, the plays in this volume revolve around painful contemporary situations. Ibsen explored the frustrations of unusually perceptive characters, each of whom falls victim to the restrictions and corruptions of a family or society against which they rebel. We see this also in Asch, Berkowitz and Hirshbein. Reading Asch's 'With the Current', or Hershbein's '*Dammerung*' or 'The Amulet', we detect the kind of destructive sexuality explored by Strindberg. And in '*Mentshn*,'

Sholem Aleichem examines the flipside of the boredom and emptiness that Chekov explored among the privileged classes.

In developing the scripts in this volume, we have highlighted the modern sensibility of each play. But we have also remained faithful to the original texts in spirit and message as we understand them. We invite theatre professionals looking for new material to bring their own creative insights to bear on these plays and, in so doing, to bring the Yiddish canon out of the wings and into the spotlight. As the number of native Yiddish speakers diminishes with each day, so does the capacity to translate into an English idiom not only the words but also the cultural heritage embodied in Yiddish plays. This volume is only one piece of an effort to accomplish the goals of *New Worlds Theatre Project* before time runs out and the literary legacy of Yiddish culture is lost forever.

References

JacobWeitzner, Sholem Aleichem in the Theatre, 1994, Farleigh Dickenson University Press.

Ruth R. Wisse, The Modern Jewish Canon, 2000, Simon and Schuster.

Encyclopedia Britannica, 'Yiddish Literature'

http://en.wikipedia.org/wiki

www.library.yale.edu/judaica/asch/aschbio.html

Key to Pronunciation of Yiddish* Words in Plays

Note: **Accent is always on the first syllable except** where accent is indicated as below with apostrophe following accented syllable.

a	'a' as in '**a**rm'
afn heykhn barg, afn griyne groz, ziytzen panes tzvey. sheyne bokhrim miyt diy frakn, kumen dort tzu zey	'fn' as in 'Pila**f n**' vegetables'; 'ey' as in '**ace**'; 'iy' as in'**fee**t'; 'o' as in 's**o**ft'; 'a' as in 'arm'; 'i' as in '**i**n'; 'u' as in 'h**oo**t'
afn lonke ferdlekh shpringn, feyglekh fliyen	'fn' as in 'Pila**f n**' vegetables'; 'e' as in 'k**e**tchup'; 'kh' as in '**ikh**, that's disgusting'; 'ey' as in '**ace**'; 'iy' as in '**fee**t'
Al naharoys' Bavel, sheym yashav'nu gam bakhiy'nu, bezakhrey'nu es Tsiyon'. Al araviym' besoykha' taliy'nu ki nohroysey'nu. Kiy shamshey lo'nu shovey'nu diyv'rey shiyr vito laley'nu siymkha' shiyru la'nu miy shiyr Tsiyyon'. (Hebrew)	'a' as in '**a**rm'; 'e' as in 'k**e**tchup'; 'ey' as in '**ace**'; 'iy' as in'**fee**t'; 'o' as in 's**o**ft'; 'a' as in '**a**rm'; 'i' as in '**i**n'; 'u' as in 'h**oo**t'; 'iy' as in '**fee**t'; 'kh' as in '**ikh**, that's disgusting'; 'r' as in sound you make when gargling
Bava Mitzi'a (Hebrew)	'a' as in '**a**rm'; 'i' as in '**i**n'
Beys Hamiyk'dash (Hebrew)	'ey' as in '**ace**'; 'a' as in '**a**rm'; 'iy' as in '**fee**t'

* Unless otherwise indicated

Borukh' ato' adowshem', Elowkey'nu melekh haolam', hamapiyl' khevley' shina al eynoy' snuma al afapoy'. umeyir' leshon bas oyin. (Hebrew)

'o' as in 's**o**ft'; 'r' as in sound you make when gargling; 'u' as in 'h**oo**t'; 'kh' as in '**ikh**, that's disgusting'; 'a' as in '**arm**'; 'ey' as in '**ace**'; 'e' as in 'k**e**tchup'; 'iy' as in 'f**ee**t'

Boyu goyim benakhlose'kho timu es eychal kod-she'kho.(Hebrew)

'u' as in 'h**oo**t'; 'i' as in '**i**n'; 'e' as in 'k**e**tchup'; 'a' as in '**arm**'; 'kh' as in '**ikh**, that's disgusting'

eylu hayeshenim', shariym' shiyr kheresh; kesheh'e' nioy'riym, shiyram mufsak (Hebrew)

'ey' as in '**ace**'; 'e' as in 'k**e**tchup'; 'iy' as in 'f**ee**t'; u' as in 'h**oo**t'; 'kh' as in '**ikh**, that's disgusting'; 'r' as in sound you make when gargling

gefal'in koyriym

'e' as in 'k**e**tchup'; 'a' as in '**arm**'; 'iy' as in 'f**ee**t'

gelt? Neyn, siz mayn talisgevald

'e' as in 'k**e**tchup'; 'ey' as in '**ace**'; 'ay' as in 'm**i**ne'; 'a' as in '**arm**'

gevald'

'e' as in 'k**e**tchup'; 'a' as in '**arm**'

ho eym im habas'

'o' as in 's**o**ft'; 'ey' as in '**ace**'; 'i' as in '**i**n'; 'a' as in '**arm**'

*Kaddish (*Hebrew)

'a' as in '**arm**'; 'i' as in '**i**n'

Kedu'she (Hebrew)

'e' as in 'k**e**tchup'; 'u' as in 'h**oo**t'

Khapun

'kh' as in '**ikh**, that's disgusting'; 'a' as in '**arm**'; 'u' as in 'h**oo**t'

Khatzois (Hebrew)

'kh' as in '**ikh**, that's disgusting'; 'a' as in '**arm**'

Khayke

'kh' as in '**ikh**, that's disgusting'; 'ay' as in 'm**i**ne'; 'e' as in 'k**e**tchup'

khazn

'kh' as in '**ikh**, that's disgusting'; 'a' as in '**arm**'; 'zn' as in '**as new**'

Khumish (Hebrew)

'kh' as in '**ikh**, that's disgusting'; 'i' as in '**i**n'

Kiyddish

'iy' as in 'f**ee**t'; 'i' as in '**i**n'

kina hore	'i' as in '**i**n'; 'a' as in '**a**rm'; 'o' as in 's**o**ft'; 'e' as in 'k**e**tchup'
kiyshke	'iy' as in 'f**ee**t'; 'e' as in 'k**e**tchup'
kohl hamla'med es ben khavey'ro toyre kiiy'lu yoldo (Hebrew)	'oh' as in 'c**oa**t'; 'a' as in '**a**rm'; 'e' as in 'k**e**tchup'; kh' as in '**ikh**, that's disgusting'; 'ey' as in '**a**ce'; 'r' as in sound you make when gargling
kohl ha sote miy darkoh shel ha am ha yehu'diy, loh ohd ekhud meytanu hu (Hebrew)	'oh' as in 'c**oa**t'; 'a' as in '**a**rm'; 'e' as in 'k**e**tchup'; 'iy' as in 'f**ee**t'; 'kh' as in '**ikh**, that's disgusting'; 'ey' as in '**a**ce'; 'r' as in sound you make when gargling; 'u' as in 'h**oo**t'
Kohl Nidrey (Hebrew)	'o' as in 's**o**ft'; 'i' as in '**i**n'; 'r' as in sound you make when gargling; 'ey' as in '**a**ce'
koyriym	'r' as in sound you make when gargling; 'iy' as in 'f**ee**t'
krosat'ke (Russian)	'o' as in 's**o**ft'; 'a' as in '**a**rm'; 'e' as in 'k**e**tchup'
kugl	'u' as in 'h**oo**t'
lo miyr avek' fun da'nent!	'o' as in 's**o**ft'; 'iy' as in 'f**ee**t'; 'r' as in sound you make when gargling; 'a' as in '**a**rm'; 'u' as in 'c**oo**k'; 'e' as in 'k**e**tchup'
makhzer (Hebrew)	'a' as in '**a**rm'; 'kh' as in '**ikh**, that's disgusting'; 'r' as in sound you make when gargling
mame	'a' as in '**a**rm'; 'e' as in 'k**e**tchup'
mameloshn	'a' as in '**a**rm'; 'e' as in 'k**e**tchup'; 'o' as in 's**o**ft'
mayn eytzer	'a' as in '**a**rm' 'ey' as in '**a**ce'; 'e' as in 'k**e**tchup'
mayn kiynd	'ay' as in 'm**i**ne'; 'iy' as in 'f**ee**t'

mentsh'(n)	'e' as in 'k**e**tchup'
Miyn hameytz'ar koro'siy ko! Miyn miyn miyn! Koro'siy koro'siy! Koro'siy ko.	'iy' as in '**fee**t'; 'a' as in '**a**rm'; 'ey' as in '**ace**'; 'o' as in 's**o**ft'
nevey'le	'e' as in 'k**e**tchup'; 'ey' as in 'ace'
Oley'nu (Hebrew)	'o' as in 's**o**ft'; 'ey' as in '**ace**; 'u' as in 'h**oo**t'
*Omeyn'. Yihey' shimey' ra'bo (*Hebrew)	'ey' as in '**ace**'; 'i' as in '**in**' 'a' as in '**a**rm'; 'o' as in 's**o**ft'
Pasku'de! A beyze yor af diyr!	'a' as in '**a**rm'; 'e' as in 'k**e**tchup'; 'ey' as in '**ace**'; 'o' as in 's**o**ft';'iy' as in 'f**ee**t'
samogon'ke (Russian)	'a' as in '**a**rm'; 'o' as in 's**o**ft'; 'e' as in 'k**e**tchup'
Shabbos	'a' as in '**a**rm'
sha shtiyl	'a' as in '**a**rm'; 'iy' as in 'f**ee**t'
shelo' som khelkey'nu kohem' v goroley'nu kichol' hamoynom' (Hebrew)	'e' as in 'k**e**tchup'; 'o' as in 's**o**ft'; 'kh' as in 'i**kh**, that's disgusting'; 'e' as in 'k**e**tchup'; 'ey' as in '**ace**'; 'u' as in 'h**oo**t'; 'r' as in sound you make when gargling; 'i' as in '**i**n'
shema' yisroyl' adonoy' elokey'new Adonoy' ekhod' (Hebrew)	'e' as in 'k**e**tchup';'a' as in '**a**rm'; 'i' as in '**in**'; 'ey' as in '**ace**'; 'o' as in 's**o**ft'; 'kh' as in 'i**kh'** that's disgusting'
shiyve	'iy' as in 'f**ee**t'; 'e' as in 'k**e**tchup'
shtetl	't' as in '**t**op'; 'e' as in 'k**e**tchup'
shteyt uf, shteyt uf. Yiydelekh. Koshere Yiydelekh, frume Yiydelekh steht uf, steht uf. lavoydas haboy'rey	'ey' as in 'ace'; 'u' as in hoot'; 'iy' as in 'feet'; 'e' as in 'ketchup'; 'kh' as in 'ikh that's disgusting'; 'r' as in sound you make when gargling
shtiykl mentsh	'iy' as in 'f**ee**t'; 'e' as in 'k**e**tchup'

siydder	'iy' as in 'f**ee**t'; 'e' as in 'k**e**tchup'; 'r' as in sound you make when gargling
tate	'a' as in '**a**rm'; 'e' as in 'k**e**tchup'
tokhter	'o' as in 's**o**ft'; 'kh' as in '**ikh**, that's disgusting'; 'e' as in 'k**e**tchup'
tvar'iyshcha (Russian)	'a' as in '**a**rm'; 'iy' as in 'f**ee**t'
ysiy'mes	'iy' as in 'f**ee**t'; 'e' as in 'k**e**tchup'
unter … viygele, shteyt a klor vays tziygele. Dos tzigele iyz gefor'en handeln. Dos vet zayn dayn baruf …	'u' as in 'h**oo**t'; 'e' as in 'k**e**tchup'; 'iy' as in 'f**ee**t' ; 'ey' as in '**a**ce'; 'a' as in '**a**rm'; 'o' as in 's**o**ft'; 'ay' as in 'm**i**ne'
va anach'nu koyriym (Hebrew)	'a' as in '**a**rm'; 'r' as in sound you make when gargling; 'iy' as in 'f**ee**t'
vos iyz diy nafke miyne? Geven" amol' Shmuel Mikhl der khazen.	'o' as in 's**o**ft'; 'iy' as in 'f**ee**t'; 'a' as in '**a**rm'; 'e' as in 'k**e**tchup'; 'kh' as in '**ikh**, that's disgusting'
Yekm Purkan	'e' as in 'k**e**tchup'; 'u' as in 'h**oo**t'; 'a' as in '**a**rm'
Yiysroeyl, af al piy shekhoto, Yiysroeyl hu	'iy' as in 'f**ee**t'; 'o' as in 's**o**ft'; 'ey' as in 'n**ai**l'; 'e' as in 'k**e**tchup'; 'a' as in '**a**rm'; ; 'u' as in 'h**oo**t'
Kiyp'per	'o' as in '**soft**'; 'iy' as in 'f**ee**t'; 'r' as in sound you make when gargling
zeyde	'ey' as in '**a**ce'; 'e' as in 'k**e**tchup'
Zhiyd	'zh' as in 'a**z**ure'; iy' as in 'f**ee**t'
Zikhor Adohshem' mey hoyo lonu habiyta urey es kherposey'nu. Nakhalosey'nu nehepkho' lizoy'riym Bohsey'nu linokhriym. somim hoyinuv'eyn ov imosey'nu ke almon'es. (Hebrew)	'i' as in '**i**n'; 'o' as in 's**o**ft'; 'a' as in '**a**rm'; 'e' as in 'k**e**tchup'; 'u' as in 'h**oo**t'; iy' as in 'f**ee**t'; 'ey' as in '**a**ce'; 'r' as in sound you make when gargling; 'kh' as in '**ikh**, that's disgusting'

Key to Pronunciation of Character Names

Note: **Accent is always on the first syllable except** where accent is indicated as below with apostrophe following accented syllable.

AKIYM	'a' as in '**a**rm'; 'iy' as in 'f**ee**t'
ALYOSH'KE	'a' as in '**a**rm'; 'e' as in 'k**e**tchup'
AVDOT'YE	'a' as in '**a**rm'; 'o' as in 's**o**ft'; 'e' as in 'k**e**tchup'
AVRUSH	'a' as in '**a**rm'; 'r' as in sound you make when gargling; 'u' as in 'c**oo**k'
BERL	'e' as in 'k**e**tchup'; 'r' as in sound you make when gargling; 'l' as in 'thrott**l**e'
BERELE	'e' as in 'k**e**tchup'; 'r' as in sound you make when gargling
DOVIYD	'o' as in 's**o**ft'; 'iy' as in 'f**ee**t'
FANITSHKE	'a' as in 'bl**o**nd'; 'e' as in 'k**e**tchup'
FIYSHL	'iy' as in 'f**ee**t'; 'shl' as in 'bu**shel**'
GIYTL	'iy' as in 'f**ee**t'; 'tl' as in 'bo**ttle**'
GOLD	'o' as in 's**o**ft'
HAVRIL'O	'a' as in '**a**rm'; 'r' as in sound you make when you gargle; 'o' as in 's**o**ft'
HERTZ	'e' as in 'k**e**tchup'
HIYMAN	'iy' as in 'f**ee**t'

KIYRL	'iy' as in 'f**ee**t'; 'r' as in sound you make when you gargle
LIYZA	'iy' as in 'f**ee**t'
MENA'SHE	'e' as in 'k**e**tchup'; 'a' as in '**a**rm'
MENDL	'e' as in 'k**e**tchup'; 'dl' as in 'bott**le**'
MEYER BER	'ey' as in '**a**ce'; 'e' as in 'k**e**tchup'; 'r' as in sound you make when you gargle
MIYRL	'iy' as in f**ee**t; 'r' as in sound you make when you gargle; 'l' as in 'thrott**le**'
MOSHKE FER-OPON'TOV	'o' as in 's**o**ft'; 'e' as in 'k**e**tchup'
NICHO'MELE	'i' as in '**i**n'; 'o' as in 's**o**ft' 'e' as in 'k**e**tchup'
NOSN	'o' as in 's**o**ft'
NODOV	'o' as in 's**o**ft'
PYATAK	'a' as in '**a**rm'
REVETSHKE	'e' as in 'k**e**tchup'
REYZL	'ey' as in '**a**ce'; 'zl' as in 'refu**sal**'
REYZELE	'ey' as in '**a**ce'; 'e' as in 'k**e**tchup'
RIYVE	'iy' as in 'f**ee**t"; 'e' as in 'k**e**tchup'
RIYVKE	'iy' as in 'f**ee**t"; 'e' as in 'k**e**tchup'
RIYKL	'iy' as in 'f**ee**t'
ROKHTCHE	'o' as in 's**o**ft'; 'kh' as in '**ikh**, that's disgusting' ; 'tch' as in '**ch**eck'; 'e' as in 'k**e**tchup'
ROKHELE	'o' as in 's**o**ft'; 'e' as in 'k**e**tchup'
SENDER	'e' as in 'k**e**tchup'
TANYE	'a' as in '**a**rm'; 'e' as in 'k**e**tchup'
TOMER	'o' as in 's**o**ft'; 'e' as in 'k**e**tchup'
YAKHNE	'a' as in '**a**rm'; 'e' as in 'k**e**tchup'

YEKHEZ'KELE	'e' as in 'k**e**tchup'; 'kh' as in '**ikh**, that's disgusting'
YAKOV	'a' as in '**a**rm'
YAYNKL	'ay' as in 'm**i**ne'; 'kl' as in 'an**kle**'
YOKHE'VED	'e' as in 'k**e**tchup'
ZIYZI	'iy' as in 'f**ee**t'
ZOREKH	'o' as in 's**o**ft'; 'e' as in 'k**e**tchup'; 'kh' as in '**ikh**, that's 'disgusting'

Glossary

Glossary of words and terms not defined within text of plays, with accented syllable followed by an apostrophe.

YIDDISH*	**ENGLISH**
Afn lonke … ferdlekh shrping'en … feglakh fliyen	In the meadow … horses leap … birds fly
Bava Metzi'a (Hebrew)	ten chapters in the *Mishne* that address legal issues concerning lost and found property, among other things
Beys Hamik'dash (Hebrew)	Holy Temple of the biblical era
gefaln' koyrim	fell prostrate during the *Oleynu* prayer
Gelt? Neyn, siz mayn ta'lisgevald.	Money? No, it's my prayer shawl bag.
gevald'!	help!
*Kaddish (*Hebrew)	mourner's prayer
Kedu'she (Hebrew)	liturgical feature consisting of a mosaic of biblical verses which is attached to the Amida, the prayer which is the central element in the three daily services

* Unless otherwise indicated

Khapun	Jewish Devil
khatzois (Hebrew)	half; used here to refer to *tikun khatzois,* service conducted by holy men at midnight to mourn the destruction of the temple and to enable its rebuilding by the coming of the messiah
Khayke	female Yiddish name used pejorativly
khazn	cantor
Khumish (Hebrew)	Torah, Five Books of Moses, Pentateuch
Kiyddish	sanctification element of liturgy, said over wine; to make *kiyddish* implies the drinking of alcohol.
kina hore	expression meaning, 'God Forbid'. Literally, may the evil eye not fall on her
kishke	stuffed derma
koyrim	we bow
Kol Nidrey (Hebrew)	Aramaic formula for Jewish dispensation of vows, recited on the eve of Yom Kippur
krosat'ke (Russian)	a beauty
kugl	pudding
Lo miyr avek' fun danent! Lo miyr avek'! …	Let's get out of here! Let's go!
makhzer (Hebrew)	prayerbook used for festivals
mame	mother
mentsh'(n)	person(s); servant(s)
mayn kind	my child
mayn eytz'er	my treasure (term of endearment)
nevey'le	carcass

Olay'nu (Hebrew)	closing prayer of the three daily services, proclaiming God as king over a united humanity
Omeyn'. Yehey' shemey' rabo (Hebrew)	Amen. Blessed be His many names. Congregation's response to cantor's recitation at certain points in prayer
Pasku'de! A beyze yor af diyr!	Bitch! Go to hell!
samogon'ke (Russian)	home-made vodka
Shabbos	Sabbath
sha shtil	quiet
shelo som khelkeynu kohem vi goroleyno kichol hamoynom (Hebrew)	who made our destiny different from the majority of people; line from *Oleynu* prayer
Shema Yisroyl	Hear O Israel; line from—and title of—prayer recited as the confession of the Jewish faith
shiva	seven; refers to the seven-day mourning period following the burial of a member of one's immediate family
shtetl	town
shtikl mentsh	reasonably decent person
siddur	prayer book
tate	father
tokhter	daughter
tvar'ishcha (Russian)	little creature
tsimes	traditional Eastern European Jewish dish; sliced carrots cooked with honey and rib beef

Unter … viygele, shteyt a klor vays tziygele. Dos Tziygele iz gefor'en handeln. Dos vet zayn dayn baruf …	"Under … cradle there lays a pure white goat. The goat went to peddle his wares. This will be your trade …;" line from Yiddish lullaby "Raisens and Almonds [*Rozhinkes Mit Mandln*]"
Va anach'nu koyrim (Hebrew)	"And we all bow down"; line in *Oleynu* prayer
Vos iz di nafke miyne? Geven' amol' Shmuel Mikhl der khazen.	Big deal! So there once was a cantor named Shmuel Mikhl.
Yehey shimey rabo	Blessed be His many names
Yekum Purkan	"May salvation rise"; title of Aramaic prayer composed in Babylonia
Yom Kiypper	Yom Kippur; Jewish Day of Atonement
zeyde	grandfather
Zhiyd	Jew

Mentshn

By Sholem Aleichem

Translated from Yiddish by Ellen Perecman and Yermiyahu Ahron Taub

Adapted by Ellen Perecman and Clay McLeod Chapman

Characters

DANIEL	An elderly bachelor who supervises the servants in Mme. Gold's household
HERTZ	A debonair servant
RIYKL	A cook
FIYSHL	Riykl's husband
LIYZA	A recently dismissed maid
REVETSHKE	A recently hired maid
FANITSHKE	A former maid in the Gold household
SENDER	Revetshke's father
YOKHEVED	Sender's wife and Revetshke's mother
MME. GOLD	*Nouveau riche,* millionaire, mistress of the house

Act One

The action takes place in a magnificent kitchen, which doubles as the servants' quarters of a very wealthy family. A staircase—prominently placed—leads upstairs to the residence. DANIEL is sitting at a small table. A red trunk is against one wall. There is a long table and chairs. HERTZ is sitting at that table writing a letter being dictated by RIYKL.

RIYKL — … Dear Sister, please write to me. Tell me about your life as a servant. Are there many servants where you work? What do they do? Let me know how they are treating you …

HERTZ — *(Writing)* "Dear Sister please write to me." … and then what?

RIYKL — There are four servants here, in addition to us. There's one just for the laundry; one for the horses; one at the front gate, and one for the garden …

HERTZ — What does she think she's doing! I've only gotten down the first few words and already she's running off like a horse without a rider!

RIYKL — Where did you leave off, dimwit?

HERTZ — I'm at … hold on. Ah! Yes! "Dear Sister."

RIYKL — That's as far as you got?

HERTZ — You think I can write it down as quickly as it comes out of your mouth? Writing is nothing like talking! There's hard work to do before putting down a single letter—and, also, I'll have you know, our boss' pen takes after its owner: it's cheap and it wobbles around.

LIYZA enters. She begins to cry.

RIYKL — *(To LIYZA)* For God's sake! Why are you crying? Has another *beys hamiykdash* been destroyed?

HERTZ — *(To LIYZA)* Out of the blue, she starts crying? You'd feel a lot better if you just went ahead and married me ...

RIYKL — Sure looks like you got a mouthful from Madame Gold! Now there's a big surprise! That's what you put up with when you're a servant!

HERTZ — Don't waste your energy thinking about them, you foolish girl ... I don't! I'm not afraid of anyone! What do I care what the boss says!? Who's Madame Gold to me? Who cares about her? Marry me, silly girl! If you did ... you'd have no more worries.

RIYKL — We've got a real one man show here, don't we? He's a matchmaker—and groom!

DANIEL enters from the staircase. HERTZ comes to attention and puts away the pen. He becomes a different person entirely. RIYKL busies herself with cooking.

DANIEL — *(To HERTZ)* Come over here, my fine young man. *(Points to LIYZA)* Well?

HERTZ — What do you mean 'well'?

DANIEL — Have you finished showing off?

HERTZ — Who?

DANIEL — Me!

HERTZ You?

DANIEL You, clown! Go upstairs, they're calling you! Damn it!!

HERTZ This very second!

HERTZ exits. DANIEL sits down, unlocks the table drawer, removes a small book, puts on a pair of glasses. He motions to LIYZA to join him at the table and opens the book.

DANIEL You're owed four months plus three weeks wages, four times eight is apparently thirty-two, and for the three weeks at two rubles a week which is three times two, so we seem to have six.. Thirty-two and six is thirty-eight. If you add twelve you get an even fifty all together … *(Hands her money)* Why are you crying? You think I miscalculated? Huh? … Don't stand on ceremony! Just take the money!

LIYZA *(Taking the money)* What? What did I do wrong? He told me I'm beautiful! He swore he loved me …

DANIEL Big deal! He loves her! That clown?

LIYZA Who are you even talking about?

DANIEL And do you know who you're talking about?

LIYZA I'm talking about Natan! Natan Moyseyeritsh …

DANIEL Wha—what did you say? Natan Moyseyeritsh?

LIYZA He …

DANIEL You foolish girl! Why did you keep it to yourself? Why didn't you tell me? You should have told me! Me! ME—damn it!

RIYKL What's going on?

DANIEL None of your business! Back to work! *(RIYKL does)* How did this happen? Tell me! You don't have to be afraid of me … You can tell me everything. He convinced you that he was in love with you? And you actually believed him? Poor girl … And here I am, thinking you'd gotten involved with that idiot! Come here. Sit down … And tell me the honest truth, now! Remember, you're talking to me … It's actually him? You're saying it's Natan Moyseyevitsh?

LIYZA Here's the ring he gave me … *(She shows him the ring on her finger)*

DANIEL Poor thing … You'll trust anybody. You kept this a secret from me?! You were seeing him … and you actually believed him? Seventh heaven, hey?! Ah, damn it! This—this is how they trick you, you poor things! What were you thinking? What on earth were you thinking? Did you really expect him to marry you? You thought you were some kind of Madame Gold?

RIYKL sneaks up on them and eavesdrops.

LIYZA When I first arrived … he followed me around. He told me I was beautiful. A really beautiful woman! That I'm an ornament for the house, that he couldn't take his eyes off me … Then he started to sigh, deep sighs, saying he loved me! He was madly in love with me! He couldn't live without me … He even asked me if I wanted to be his one and only … Asked me to take pity on him! Promising me that he would persuade them. If they wouldn't allow it, he'd poison himself. Or shoot himself … He'd commit suicide, one way or another.

DANIEL Did he care about you? What did he tell you today? Yesterday? The day before yesterday? Did you speak to him?

LIYZA What? You think I didn't speak to him? I told him everything … and cried.

DANIEL She cried … She cried! And what did he do?

LIYZA He asked me—nicely, mind you—to please be quiet about the whole thing. He promised me gifts, money

... And when I refused the gifts, he got angry! He told me if I make a scandal, it'd be worse for me, for my sister ...

DANIEL Sister? How does he know about her?

LIYZA So I told him that I have a sister ... She works in a store as a cashier. If word gets out about all this, she'll lose her job ...

DANIEL How did I miss all this! ... And why didn't you tell me sooner, you poor thing! What other relatives do you have in town besides your sister?

LIYZA Only my sister. She's younger than me.

DANIEL Don't worry. Nothing will happen to your sister ... But it's a good thing you told me. I'll see to it straight away ... I'll give you a note to take to an acquaintance of mine. You'll stay there until I figure out what to do. I'll see to this ... *(Takes out a small piece of paper)*

From the top of the staircase MME. GOLD's voice calls, "Daniel! Daniel!"

DANIEL *(Hiding the piece of paper in the table drawer)* In a minute! In a minute!

DANIEL exits up the stairs.

RIYKL You think I didn't hear? I hear everything! That's the life of a servant. To hell with them all—all the rich!

LIYZA Oh, dear Riykl—I'm in trouble! What'll I do? Where will I go? What will I tell people?

RIYKL Don't cry, silly girl! Now you know how much I hate meddling in other people's business ... But if this happened to me, if such a thing happened to me, I would squeeze the life out of them! I'd skin them alive. Skin them alive! That should teach their grandchildren not to treat servants like that!

LIYZA My sister will lose her job! What will I do? What will I do?

RIYKL Here's your chance to gain some security with a dowry! They have enough. It's okay … Let them suffer! And find a husband, foolish girl. Believe me—it'd be a good thing. Get married and give up being a servant. Become a lady in charge of your own servants … Think about it! Oh, someone's coming!

DANIEL and HERTZ enter from the staircase.

HERTZ They'll use any excuse! Totally trumped up charges!!

DANIEL Quiet! *(To LIYZA)* Did you pack up your things? *(Opens the table drawer)* No, here's another fifty. You'll get more besides this for expenses. I'll see to it. Poor things! Lost sheep, God's creatures! Damn it! *(LIYZA starts to leave*) Take your time. I'll give you a note; I'll give you a letter.

RIYKL You know that I hate meddling in other people's business, but now she has an opportunity to get some security. At least a dowry … Such a foolish creature we've got here!

DANIEL Who's asking you for advice? You belong at the stove! Prepare the table for three people. Madame Gold's relatives, her poor relations, are coming any minute now. They'll have to be fed in the kitchen along with the servants …

HERTZ At least it's not with the dogs …

SENDER, YOKHEVED and REVETSCHKE enter from the staircase. SENDER has lots of facial hair.

RIYKL What's this?

HERTZ Oh my … A full harvest on this guy's face. Nice and overgrown!

DANIEL — Sit down here at the table, we'll give you something to eat … Riykl! Give them something to eat!

SENDER washes his hands and then loudly recites the blessing over bread; HERTZ responds "Omeyn yehey shemey rabo" … RIYKL stifles a laugh. MADAME GOLD enters from the staircase. As she does, there is a commotion in the kitchen. RIYKL throws herself at the oven; HERTZ snatches a plate, bangs forks, throws spoons. LIYZA rises and exits. DANIEL takes off his glasses and hunches over so that he appears shorter. SENDER throws food.

MADAME GOLD — *(Standing on the lowest step)* Riykl! Give them something to eat. And some tea. *(To YOKHEVED)* I completely forgot to ask, what's your daughter's name?

YOKHEVED — Riyve …

SENDER — That's Riyvke!

MADAME GOLD — Riyve? Riyvke? That's not very attractive! Reveke, Rebetshke … We'll call her Revetshke.

YOKHEVED — If you prefer Revetshke. I can't tell you what to do. She's yours now.

SENDER — Exactly what I said! As long as she's happy and has everything she needs. It's not what you think—it's what you do.

MADAME GOLD — That depends on her. If she behaves, all will go well for her. If she misbehaves … things will go poorly.

DANIEL — *(Mimicing her)* If she's a good servant, all will go well for her. If she's a bad servant, things will go poorly.

HERTZ and RIYKL — *(In unison)* If she's a good servant, all will go well for her. If she's a bad servant, things will go poorly.

HERTZ — *(Aside)* I hope things go poorly for them!

MADAME GOLD — My servants have never complained about me.

DANIEL Our servants never complain.

HERTZ and RIYKL *(In unison)* Never complain? *(Aside)* Screw them!

MADAME GOLD In my house, when there is a birthday, I give all the servants gifts.

DANIEL Here all the servants get gifts!

HERTZ and RIYKL *(In unison)* We get gifts all the time!

HERTZ *(Aside)* So they'll have everything they need!

REVETSHKE Why gifts? Gifts aren't necessary …

YOKHEVED Riyvele, what are you doing? Hush!

SENDER Exactly what I was going to say! Silence is golden …

HERTZ *(Aside)* It sounds like this guy is speaking Aramaic …

MADAME GOLD And it's a good thing she knows how to write! Sometimes they need to write lists of items in the attic … People carry things off, you know. They steal …

DANIEL Steal!

HERTZ and RIYKL And how they steal!

HERTZ *(Aside)* Poor thieves!

MADAME GOLD *(To REVETSHKE)* Eat up and get to work. Daniel! Have a look at the horses, see if they've been fed or if the oats are rotting. They love to write invoices …

MADAME GOLD exits. The mood changes entirely. DANIEL puts on his glasses and stands up straight, then sits down in his chair and writes. RIYKL goes to the table. The guests eat. HERTZ eats with them. At the top of the stairs, a voice calls "Daniel! Daniel! … DANIEL takes off his glasses, hunches over, and goes toward the staircase.

DANIEL Right away! Right away! I'm coming! Coming!

DANIEL climbs up the stairs and exits.

RIYKL	Eat, my dear guests!
YOKHEVED	Who is this sinister man? That one, there. The one they call 'Daniel'? One minute he's self-important and the next minute he's meeker than a mouse.
HERTZ	That's our supervisor.
SENDER	Your … what?
RIYKL	He's the steward. He's in charge of all the servants. All of our orders come through him. Are you close relatives of Madame Gold?
YOKHEVED	Not very close. But we're friendly.
SENDER	Second in third. You want to know how? Here, I'll explain it to you.
HERTZ	I suppose it's worth knowing. A person should know everything that goes on in the world—don't you agree?
SENDER	My uncle … Well, actually—the uncle of both of us, since my wife and I are cousins, was related to Madame Gold's aunt's sister and brother. Follow me?
YOKHEVED	Quite the opposite! Our aunt and Madame Gold's uncle were sister and brother.
SENDER	Exactly what I said!
HERTZ	*(To YOKHEVED)* What did he say?
YOKHEVED	You said that our uncle and her mother …
SENDER	Why would I say that?
HERTZ	*(To YOKHEVED)* How could he say such a thing?
YOKHEVED	*(To her daughter)* Didn't he say that, Riyvele?
REVETSHKE	Why does it matter what he said? Just go ahead and eat. You haven't eaten all day …
HERTZ	*(To SENDER)* Your daughter is right, believe me! You can't dance on an empty stomach. So … you're relatives, right? They actually … invited you to visit?

SENDER: Oh no! Not at all … We came on our own. To look for a position for our daughter. We remembered that we have wealthy relatives in the area, so we came by. At first they didn't even recognize us …

YOKHEVED: Why would they know us? They're so rich, good for them! Millionaires!

A bell rings from the top of the stairs.

HERTZ: Can't they even let a man eat in peace? We're like dogs! Grab a bite and choke it down. I wish they'd choke!

HERTZ ascends the staircase and exits.

RIYKL: *(To YOKHEVED)* So I guess you really are …

YOKHEVED: What did you think? We are very respectable people …

REVETSHKE: Why do they need to know about our family? Are you marrying me off?

YOKHEVED: Why not? We don't want them to think that you're a servant just like all the other servants …

REVETSHKE: Mother! It was hard to accept that I was going to be a servant, but now that I'm here I'm just like everyone else …

REVETSHKE finishes her meal and gets to work washing and drying dishes.

SENDER: *(After reciting the blessing)* Hmm … True, true. Please have mercy on the earth and on our food!

LIYZA enters and makes herself at home.

REVETSHKE: Who's that?

RIYKL: That's our former chambermaid. She was just fired.

REVETSHKE Why?

YOKHEVED They fired a servant. No big deal! They hire, they fire!

SENDER *(Picks up in the middle of the blessing after meals, then)* Hmm … Mmm. The merciful creator!

RIYKL *(To YOKHEVED)* What is your husband saying?

YOKHEVED It's from the Talmud. You wouldn't understand.

DANIEL enters from the staircase.

DANIEL *(To LIYZA)* Poor thing! Damn it, you should have said something earlier! Come here. *(He goes back to the letter)* Here is her address … Go see her. And give my regards. Tell her that I might still get there today, if I can. If not, then tomorrow …

LIYZA goes to a red trunk, opens it, searches for something, then locks it back up.

SENDER *(To DANIEL)* How do you do? I hear that you're the second in command?

DANIEL Your point?

SENDER Nothing. Nothing … I just wanted to ask you to look after our daughter. You know—keep an eye on her.

DANIEL Look after her? Keep an eye on her? Oh, yes. I'll keep an eye on her all right!

YOKHEVED She's our precious child … She's not an only child, thank God. But she's our oldest and brightest. Please look after her.

REVETSHKE No one has to look after me! I can take care of myself just fine …

YOKHEVED *(To her daughter)* Foolish girl! *(To DANIEL)* You do understand. An attractive girl amongst strangers …

DANIEL — An attractive girl amongst strangers ... Yes. Yes. Definitely one of the benefits.

REVETSHKE — Don't worry about me, Mother. No one's snatching me away. I'm not ten years old ...

YOKHEVED — *(To RIYKL)* Isn't she something? *(To her husband)* Sender, put your coat on. We should go. *(To her daughter)* Take good care of yourself, Riyvele. With God's help ... you'll be better off here than at home.

SENDER — That's what I was going to say. Everything depends on luck. *(To DANIEL)* Take care, Daniel ... And look after the child.

DANIEL — I'll look after your child ... Yes. I'll look after her.

SENDER and YOKHEVED exit up the staircase. REVETSCHKE sees them out and then returns. HERTZ is not far behind her.

HERTZ — Madame would like a wagon harnessed so that our Liyza can leave honorably. *(To DANIEL)* And Natan Moyseyevitsh wants to see you about the horses.

DANIEL — Again about the horses! He's already nagged me to death about the horses! A horse is more valuable to them than a servant!

DANIEL exits up the stairs.

HERTZ — Ha ha! The best morsel goes to the worst dog ... *(To LIYZA)* You didn't want to marry me, huh? My pedigree wasn't good enough for you! Because I'm one of the servants? Think about it. If the servants started marrying the rich and the rich started marrying the servants, just imagine what the world look like?

RIYKL — *(To HERTZ)* Maybe you'd better keep your mouth shut, you heretic! This poor girl is so unhappy ... and here he comes with that glib tongue of his!

LIYZA *(Crying on RIYKL's shoulder)* My dear mother …

REVETSHKE *(To HERTZ)* Why is she crying?

HERTZ She just remembered something sad.

REVETSHKE *(To RIYKL)* What's with all the sobbing?

RIYKL Her spirits are low, so she's crying!

REVETSHKE *(To LIYZA)* What's the matter? Tell me …

LIYZA Oh, I hope God above watches over you—and that what happened to me never happens to you! *(To RIYKL)* Mama! You were like a mother to me!

RIYKL Enough. Enough crying, my child! It's in God's hands now. Have a safe trip … I hope your wishes come true.

HERTZ *(Carrying LIYZA's trunk)* My goodness. She sure has packed a lot into this trunk …

HERTZ carries the trunk offstage, with LIYZA following.

RIYKL This is how a servant gets treated! Servants and dogs—they treat both like dirt! Well, it's her own fault. A servant should remember that she's nothing more than that! *(To REVETSHKE)* Hear that, young lady? When you get there *(She gestures upstairs)*, keep in mind that you're a servant and this is where you belong …

HERTZ comes down the staircase.

HERTZ One servant down! *(To RIYKL)* Just one thing bothers me, though. Isn't it enough that they do something wrong, but then they go and blame it on someone else …

REVETSHKE Was she caught stealing?

RIYKL You're just a silly goose!

HERTZ Silly—but smart, from what I can tell. I love girls like that!

HERTZ goes to touch REVETSHKE's face.

RIYKL — No hands! You're not Natan Moyseyevitsh …

HERTZ — They can do anything they want, while we can't do anything.

RIYKL — They're rich—we are servants.

HERTZ — I haven't held my guitar for so long, my fingers have gotten stiff. Damn it! *(He takes a guitar out from under his bed)* When you're down, you have to drive away these sad thoughts … Play a merry tune. What should I play? When you hear me play, you'll forgive me for anything! I'd be very pleased if all the beautiful girls and all the beautiful women would listen to me play … Well, Riykl? What should I sing, what do you want to hear?

RIYKL — Something in Yiddish?

HERTZ — A Yiddish song? Ok, I'll do *Yekum Purkan* for you. *(Sings and plays an upbeat melody) Yekum purkon …*

As the music progresses, RIYKLl's husband, FIYSHL, enters. Everyone is so caught up in the music they fail to notice him.

FIYSHL — Certainly is lively in here … Are you celebrating some holiday …?!

HERTZ — Everyday's a holiday! We have nothing to do, so we're just biding our time.

FIYSHL — You just fritter away your time like this? *(To his wife)* Aren't you going to ask about our child? All you need is a guitar and a lazy bum to strum it!

RIYKL — Sit down, rest.

FIYSHL — *(To HERTZ)* Out with it! What are you doing, fooling around with my wife? Entertaining her with your little ditties?

HERTZ — First off—I'm not entertaining only your wife. She doesn't rate that. And second—let's not forget that among servants, there is no such thing as husband, wife, sister, or brother.

FIYSHL — That so? You belong to no one?

HERTZ — What do you think? You frolicking pauper! It's a free country!

RIYKL — *(To her husband)* I know what this idiot will tell you!

FIYSHL — What do you mean—idiot? He's no idiot! A womanizer, yes! A player, most definitely. A ladies' man, first and foremost. A rascal after anything that wears a skirt …

HERTZ — Is it my fault that all women want me as their plaything?

RIYKL — You can be everybody's teddy bear for all I care, fool!

HERTZ — The things that go on up there! What I've seen going on upstairs—my goodness! There's no such thing as a husband, a wife—mine and yours. Everything is shared! What more evidence do you need? I saw someone embrace the Madame! Look here …

HERTZ goes to demonstrate by extending his arms towards RIYKL.

RIYKL — Like hell you will!

DANIEL enters from upstairs.

DANIEL — *(To HERTZ)* You won't know what hit you! Go upstairs. They're calling you, damn it!

HERTZ — *(To FIYSHL)* Take care! Have fun!

HERTZ goes up the staircase.

FIYSHL *(To HERTZ)* Go to hell! And I hope you fall on your ass along the way!

DANIEL sits down at his table and begins to arrange money in a few piles.

DANIEL *(To FIYSHL)* You shouldn't let yourself get so worked up by that crazy clod. His words have about as much substance as a dog's bark.

DANIEL opens the table drawer and removes the payroll books.

FIYSHL Does a servant have the value of a human being as far as they're concerned? You're their property. You get no Sabbath, no holidays! You can't see your wife or child. And if you ever manage to find a way to see your wife—you find a guy like this! That charlatan over there—strumming on his guitar with people looking at him, as if he's God's gift to mankind!

DANIEL Nonsense …

RIYKL What do you have to say to that?

FIYSHL To you—it's nonsense. To me—it's painful! A servant is still a person. A person with drive. Ambition!

DANIEL Ambition? What kind? A servant with ambitions! A servant has no right to have ambitions?

RIYKL *(To DANIEL)* What do you say to that? Ambition!

FIYSHL Yes, ambition! You heard me. We may be nothing more than servants—but servants have souls, too! All week long, we're harnessed like mules. Whenever we find a half hour to visit our children or our wives—we get into trouble with you know who! *(He unwraps a shawl from paper and gives it to RIYKL)* Here—I bought you a shawl. Cost me only three groshen …

RIYKL I'll give it to Feygele. Poor thing, she has nothing to keep her warm … I saw her the other week in the market. She didn't look very happy … Terrible to be raising a child while you're a servant. We don't even have control over our own lives!

FIYSHL You could think about spending more time with her. Do you have time for that? Or are you steering clear? Maybe she can come see you! You shouldn't drift away from your own child.

RIYKL He's rebuking me! Drifting away from my child? The Madame won't stand to hear anything about our children. The Madame despises servants who have children!

FIYSHL They despise everyone! She'd be better off if you brought her here, get her a job as a servant here so she can be with you …

RIYKL A servant here? Oh—I hope I never see that day, dear God! I'd never give my child away to these wolves. What happened to Fanitshke and Liyza will never happen to her!

FIYSHL *(Directing this upstairs)* I hope you burn in hell seventeen times over!

A woman's voice is heard from above calling "Daniel! Daniel?"

DANIEL *(Shrinking)* I'm coming! I'm coming! *(Aside)* Up and down! Up and down! Damn it.

DANIEL exits up the stairs.

FIYSHL It's the same everywhere! … Over at my place they're already looking for me: "Fiyshl!" In every direction: "Fiyshl! Fiyshl"! Fiyshl should tell them all where they can go! I hope they want to live this life as much as we want to get away from it … Oh! Oh! Oh! Just because you're a servant, does that mean you've sold yourself? A husband is torn from his wife, a mother from her children, a sister from her brothers … It's disgusting! Such a rotten world! *(To REVETSHKE)* Do you hear me, young lady? You're probably the new chambermaid, yes? Someday you'll get married … I only hope you won't remain a servant after the wedding! Better to go hungry than to be a married servant. *(To RIYKL)* And you? Wouldn't hurt you to keep your distance from the musician who fancies himself a real somebody, would it? See you!

FIYSHL exits. RIYKL starts laughing.

REVETSHKE Are you laughing?

RIYKL Would you rather I cry?

REVETSHKE Isn't your husband right?

RIYKL Who said he wasn't?

REVETSHKE Why do you upset him?

RIYKL Me? What can I do? It's my fault we're both slaves? When I was a girl, I was a servant. I collected a dowry—then I married him. No point in staying home now. He'd always be a servant—and I would sit like a lady with absolutely nothing to do. So I got myself another job as a servant. And when my Feygele grew up, I got her a job as a servant too …

REVETSHKE As a servant?

RIYKL As a servant. We're servants and our children are servants and our children's children will probably be servants. It's God's will that we should all be servants.

REVETSHKE It's our destiny to be servants?

RIYKL Undeniably. Take yourself, for example. You are now a servant here. You'll earn a few rubles. You'll probably marry a servant …

REVETSHKE What?

RIYKL A servant.

REVETSHKE Servants only marry other servants?

RIYKL Who else is there?

HERTZ descends the staircase carrying a bundle.

HERTZ Down, up! Up, down! I got some beating from her! Daniel wasn't fooled either! First from him, then from her … Up and down! Up and down! (*Untying the bundle)* Up and down! Down and up!

RIYKL Why are you going on about them today!

HERTZ They can all go to hell for all I care! Up and down! Down and up! Now they're expecting guests. The Krakovetskis should be here soon. Mother and daughter. Up and down! Down and up! Natan Moyseyevitsh got all dolled up. Everyone's expecting an engagement! Up and down! Down and up! *(To REVETSHKE)* Don't you have any work to do? Why are you just sitting there? My dear girl, help me with these! Come on, kitty cat! Our Madame hates it when you sit there like a lady. She says that sitting is positively unhealthy for a servant. *(Pinching Revetshke's cheek)* Cheeks like dough!

RIYKL How dare you, you scoundrel! He think she's Liyza!

FANITSHKE enters unnoticed. She is all dressed up in fancy clothes and lots of make up.

HERTZ We have to break her in slowly. Before she goes upstairs and before Natan Moyseyevitsh gets to her … *(Noticing FANITSHKE)* Hold everything! It's Fanitshke! What a surprise!

FANITSHKE *Bonjour, Madame*!

RIYKL Well I'll be, a real lady! Fanitshke! Why don't we ever see you? Afraid to show your face all this time? Where have you been?

HERTZ Ten questions at once? Let her catch her breath! *(He brings Fanitschke a chair)*

FANITSHKE *(To HERTZ) Merci beaucoup*! *(Curtsies to him)*

HERTZ You speak French now?

FANITSHKE *(Laughs)* Now I speak only French: *Bonjour, je vous pri, qu'est que c'est, donnez-moi quel' que chose, au revoir, l'argent, messieurs,*—eh? Did you understand what I said? You're looking at me and you're in complete shock? This isn't the old Fanitshke … Fanitshke is not a servant any more! I'm a servant only to myself! *Voila! (Points to her pocket and laughs. Then to REVETSHKE)* Why are looking at me like that? Who the hell are you? A new chambermaid?? Where is Liyza? Canned again? *(Laughs)* I'm better off than any of you … I have a house with four rooms and a kitchen, *parole de honneur*. A closet full of clothes and jewelry *quel'que magnifique*! I just got robbed of a pair of diamond earrings. Really, it was my fiancé … a dark handsome stranger with burning eyes *(Laughs)* Just look at the way she's looking at me! …

RIYKL *(To HERTZ)* She looks too happy to me!

HERTZ I think she's been drinking.

FANITSHKE *Ce n'est pas vrai*! I haven't been drinking. I don't drink whiskey; I drink wine! *Champagne, parole de honneur. (She takes out a cigarette, which HERTZ lights for her)*

HERTZ So? You have a fiance, Fanitshke?

FANITSHKE What do you mean "Fanitshke"? I'm not Fanitshke anymore! Fania Yefimovna, what the hell! All the officers, colonels, and generals know me only as Fania Yefimovna *i basta*! … Two students got into a fight over

Fania Yefimovna, *parole de honneur*! They also hit me, you see? *(She rolls up her sleeve to reveal a blue mark)* Look! *(Laughs)*

RIYKL — Just tell us, child—where have you been all this time? Why don't we ever see you?

FANITSHKE — What more can I tell you? I've told you everything! But what goes on here? *(Points to her heart)* That is no one's business! *(Laughs)* … And upstairs, what's going on up there? They fired Liyza and hired this one? They fire and they hire … There are always new servants. Always new servants! *(Laughs)* Servants! *(Laughs)* What's with all the long faces? Why look at me like that? Because I'm laughing? It's good for me to laugh! They should have it as good as I do! *(She indicates upstairs)*

HERTZ — Amen.

FANITSHKE — Even half as good!

HERTZ — Amen and praise the Lord!

FANITSHKE — I have them to thank for what I have now! No day, no night. Always decked out, made up. Always happy! And look at my brother … He had to leave here in shame. Gone, no one knows where. Some people think that he's in … *(Whispering)* That he's a revolutionary. He used to be too quiet—now he's a revolutionary! The shame of it all, such a headache … *(Pause)* He loved me once! Loved me! Loved me! *(Her laughter turns to tears)*

REVETSHKE — Come now. Don't cry …

FANITSHKE — *(To REVETSHKE)* Get away from me! Don't touch me! You're a saint! I'll contaminate you! *(Laughs)* Just like my fiancé says … My fiancé is a poet. He writes me poems!

HERTZ — She has so many fiancés!

FANITSHKE — So many fiancés? You wanted to marry me, *mon cher ami* … Mr. Fancy Pants. Come here, *s'il vous plait*! *(She grabs HERTZ and starts dancing with him)*

MADAME GOLD enters from upstairs with DANIEL behind her. She stands on the steps for a moment and then recognizes FANITSHKE.

MADAME GOLD What's going on here? What's going on in my own kitchen? My servants are indulging themselves in such … Daniel! I want all the servants fired! Do you hear me? All the servants!!

DANIEL All the servants. All the servants! …

FANITSHKE Fire all the servants? It's so easy for you to hire and fire servants! You throw out servants like they're garbage, *ma chère madame*! If I can help it, it's *au revoir avec plaisir*! *(Curtsies to her)* Regards to your honest-to-goodness brat, Natan Moyseyevitsh. We'll run into him again … You really shouldn't toss your servants out into the street, Madame. Servants are also people, damn it!

MADAME GOLD Daniel! Don't just stand there like some clod! Throw her out! Throw them all out! All of them! All the servants! Damn them to hell! Damn the servants! You're wreaking havoc on my house! You're defiling my halls!!….

DANIEL takes money, papers and books out of the table drawer and throws it at MADAME GOLD's feet along with keys to the house.

DANIEL Enough! I've been silent long enough, damn it! *(To the servants)* You're ruining their house! You're destroying their house! We servants are ruining their house! Get your coats. Let's go! Let's get out of here! We shouldn't be here! Who are we? What are we? We're lower than the low. We're nothing! We're God knows what! We're servants! People! *Mentshn* …

CURTAIN

Carcass (Neveyle)

By Peretz Hirshbein

Translated from Yiddish by Ellen Perecman and Mark Altman

Adapted by Ellen Perecman, Mark Altman and Clay McLeod Chapman

Characters

AVRUSH	A former horse trader
SHPRIYNTZE	Avrush's first wife
BRAYNE	Avrush's second wife
REYZL	Brayne's daughter
BERL	Reyzl's suitor
MENDL	Son of Avrush and Shpriyntze
NIKHOME	Daughter of Avrush and Shpriyntze
GIYTL	Shpriyntze's friend

Act One

AVRUSH's home. A one-room basement apartment with one small window. The apartment is always dark. There are two beds. A broken table and a few chairs. On the wall a few pictures without frames. A Spring night. A single small lamp provides the only light.

AVRUSH is lying on one bed, drunk, fully clothed, snoring. REYZL sits on the other bed. Her hair is unruly. Her clothes just hang on her frame. She is wearing torn galoshes on her feet. She takes a letter out of her pocket and tries to read it by the light of the lamp. AVRUSH lifts up his head and sneezes. REYZL hides the letter.

AVRUSH Huh? What did you say?

REYZL Nobody's talking to you.... He's dreaming.

AVRUSH Where's your *mame*? Did she finally get what's coming to her? Your *mame* is a harpy sent to hound me. Your *mame*.... Where the hell did she go, your *mame*? Where?

REYZL doesn't answer. She hums a melody under her breath.

AVRUSH Why are you wasting kerosene for no good reason?

REYZL Can't you sleep?

AVRUSH Tell your *mame* … Tell her … Tell … *(He begins to snore again)*

BERL enters cautiously.

BERL Aha! The baby-doll is home. You were waiting for me, weren't you?

BERL takes REYZL's hand.

REYZL *(Pulling her hand away)* Don't squeeze my hand so hard!

BERL Reyzele … Berl doesn't like to play games. Give me your hand. Don't be afraid. I won't squeeze it any more, I promise. It isn't bleeding yet. Here—give it to me. I'll kiss it—and make it better.

REYZL You don't care.

BERL *(Kissing the tips of REYZL' fingers)* Ah how sweet, how sweet! *(Counting her fingers)* One, two, three—Baby Doll! You'd like a ring for your finger, wouldn't you?

REYZL Buy it and you'll see.

BERL *(Lifts up Reyzl's ring finger)* How would you like it on this finger?

REYZL Buy it and you'll see.

BERL A simple band without a stone.

REYZL Buy it and you'll see.

BERL looks at REYZL earnestly.

REYZL Why are you so serious all of a sudden?

BERL Baby Doll, if only you'd seen me pummel these two guys …

REYZL Today?

BERL Just this morning.

REYZL Why?

BERL They asked for it, that's why.

REYZL Let's get back to the part where you were talking about buying me that thing you were talking about …

BERL You're mocking me …

REYZL Buy it and you'll see!

BERL To hell with them. Did they say anything about me? They can just drop dead for all I care …

REYZL Are you angry at me? *(BERL is silent)* Berl?

BERL "Berl *Khazer*, Berl the Pig." I see … They insult me and it doesn't bother you one bit.

REYZL What about the ring, huh? Tell me … *(Silence)* Berele … Do you write your own letters? Do you even know how to write?

BERL Me? … I can write. Of course I can write!

REYZL You have beautiful handwriting. *(Taking letter out of her pocket)* Is this your handwriting, Berele? Berele?

BERL I swear I know how to write. To hell with them!

REYZL Who are you cursing?

BERL It doesn't matter who I'm cursing. I will curse and—and then I'll split their skulls open! I'll burn them alive! *(Beat)* Did you read it?

REYZL It's difficult to read your handwriting. Here. Read me what you wrote.

BERL Why should I?

REYZL I want to know what you wrote. Your name there—Berl—I recognized that right away. Opening it I saw that. Here—right?

BERL *(Handing her the letter)* You know very well what's written there … Don't you, Reyzele?

REYZL You want to be a good sport for once, Berl?

BERL Who told you I'm a bad sport?

REYZL No one. I'm just asking …

BERL For you?

REYZL For me.

BERL For you … Berl will do anything. Whatever Reyzl asks.

REYZL See how I'm barefoot?

BERL Don't you have some shoes?

REYZL I don't. My *mame* sold them. Maybe she hid them.

BERL Why?

REYZL So I can't leave the house. And I would never leave the house in these ugly things.

BERL Your *mame* can just go to hell for all I care.

REYZL So what about …?

BERL You want some shoes—I'll get you some shoes …

REYZL With heels?

BERL Even heels if that's what you want.

REYZL Expensive shoes?

BERL *(Taking out his wallet)* Look—look at all this money! Plenty enough for shoes, too.

REYZL Where did you get so much money?

BERL Take it if you want it.

REYZL All of it?

BERL All of it. It's Berl! Don't you understand? I am Berl *Khazer*! I … I have money. I have everything, everything … I am Berl the Pig! Reyzl, tell me … want that diamond ring now?

REYZL Where are you going to get one?

BERL I can get one if I want. Do you want it? Just say so and it's yours …

AVRUSH wakes up and sits up.

REYZL Look what we have here.

BERL Ah, Avrush!

AVRUSH mumbles unintelligibly.

BERL How many times did you make *kiyddish* today?

AVRUSH Berl?

BERL Don't you recognize me?

AVRUSH I recognized you … I recognized you. *(Mumbles unintelligibly)* She's not here yet?

BERL Who are you waiting for?

AVRUSH For the curse of my life! For my shrew! *(BERL and REYZL are playful with each other)* Her *mame*—that's who! Berl? Are you falling for her? Are you … She is no better than her *mame*! I hope they both get swallowed up by the earth on the very same day. Both in the same day! She thinks she wears the pants in the family. She supports me. *(Laughs)* She supports me! Can you believe that? Before I met her I was starving. Starving! Can you believe that? What do you think about that, huh? What does that make me? As far as I'm concerned … I am the same Avrush I was 20 years ago. Twenty years ago, as I live and breathe! This is the same Avrush they called "Sir." "Sir!" As I stand here! My horses were priceless. As I live and breathe! Herds of horses. As sure as I stand here … Officers rode my horses … Generals!

As sure as I stand here—generals! I was not starving then, was I? What do you have to say about that Berl? Take a look at her … Like mother, like daughter. *Ho eym im ha bas.* As it says in the *Shabbos* song …

REYZL Is that a dog barking?

AVRUSH What disrespect! Did you hear that Berl, did you hear? I told you! No better than her *mame*! *(Sits down on the bed and talks to himself)* My best years—all gone! Up in smoke, just like a dream. *(Mumbles unintelligibly)* Like a dream …

BERL Come with me, Avrush. Let me buy you a drink …

REYZL Poor thing. He hasn't had a drop to drink all day …

AVRUSH See Berl. She's barefoot! Her own *mame* sold her shoes! You should have killed her!

BERL Excuse me?

AVRUSH You know my daughter. My Nikhomele? Now there's a child! Intelligent. Beautiful! Educated! I was driven out of the Garden of Eden. Driven out, I tell you … Now my daughter avoids me. I never see her. And look what I have here! My Nikhomele! What a beauty—a princess! As I live and breathe!

BERL Avrush, Abba …? *(To REYZL)* He's crying now! *(To AVRUSH)* This doesn't become you …

AVRUSH What do you think? The beast owns me now. I fell into this … My own daughter avoids me. Not long ago I saw her … She was walking home from school with her girlfriends. They were marching like some regiment of soldiers. Probably didn't even see me. But I recognized her. I'm her father after all … And see? I've been sold a bill of old goods!

BERL Come on. Let's go wet our whistles.

REYZL Where are you going?

BERL You know where I'm going.

REYZL And the shoes?

BERL I'll be back with your shoes …

BRAYNE is a ragamuffin. She enters carrying two baskets.

AVRUSH Now I'm stuck! I …

BRAYNE And where do think you're going this late? *(Noticing BERL, she changes her tone)* Good evening! Oh, I have no strength left … I can't even feel my hands. What a day! So long … As long as in the summer. They can all go to hell! Wearing me down like this. Where are you going at this hour? You'll come banging on the door in the middle of the night again …? You sure are some blessing from God—aren't you?

BERL Brayne—why break his balls?

BRAYNE I can't stand the thought of him, that's why! There's no place on earth for people like him … *(To REYZL)* Why are you sitting there doing nothing?

REYZL What do you want from me?

BRAYNE I'll show you what …

BERL exits whistling.

BRAYNE *(To REYZL)* I'll kill you! I'll take all your clothes away if I have to. I'll leave you naked! *(We hear people shouting at each other through the door)* Who's out there?

MENDL *(Rushing into the house with a sack)* That bastard. I hope he drops dead! He almost strangled me!

BRAYNE Always getting into fights. Scares me to death!

AVRUSH Mendl?

MENDL What if it is?

AVRUSH Mendl!

MENDL What?

BRAYNE What do you think it is that he wants? Money for booze—that's what!

MENDL If I want to give it to him I'll give it to him. I don't have to ask for your permission.

BRAYNE As far as I'm concerned you can do whatever the hell you want …

AVRUSH *(Goes to the sack, opens it and looks inside)* You skinned this yourself?

REYZL He dragged another animal hide into our house!

AVRUSH *(To REYZL)* You're a *neveyle*—that's what you are! *(To MENDL)* This is worth a good five rubles.

REYZL Soon he'll be bringing a dead horse into our house!

MENDL Well, look who thinks she's a little princess. What a princess! The barefoot contessa!

BRAYNE *(To REYZL)* What's Berl *Khazer* doing here?

REYZL Hell if I know.

BRAYNE Don't talk that way to me! I'll kill you! Do you hear me, you little bitch?

REYZL Give me back my shoes!

BRAYNE I'll take your shirt too! I'll leave and lock you inside. You'll learn to treat your *mame* with respect, if it kills me! Your *tate*'s dead. Now I can do as I please.

MENDL Reyzl! I'll buy you a pair of shoes. If you want them, just say the word …

BRAYNE And I'll buy you all broken bones!

MENDL *(Carries his sack over to AVRUSH)* See *Tate*? This is some hide!

REYZL Put it down! I'm gonna split your head open! Try taking that hide out of the sack!

AVRUSH Insolent!

MENDL Get out of here, you barefoot bitch!

AVRUSH Pay no attention to her, son. She's no better than her *mame*. This is worth at least 5 rubles.

BRAYNE Look who I'm wasting my life with!

MENDL Oh, so fragile … My little princess! This hide is cleaner than you and your *mame* put together!

AVRUSH Oh, my Nikhomele … Driven out of the Garden of Eden! I've been driven out! She avoids me like the plague. Have you seen Nikhomele? *(MENDL does not respond)* Yes? Mendl!

MENDL Leave me alone!

AVRUSH gets up and turns off the lamp.

BRAYNE Just because you're so dim … Drunk! It's not dark enough in the house? Why are you turning off the light?

AVRUSH It's not like we're doing anything anyway …

BRAYNE Save your money for booze!

AVRUSH Leech! Vampire!

BRAYNE I should feed you? Feed you to the worms! I don't know what's become of you … What was I just doing?

REYZL exits.

BRAYNE And where do you think you're going now? Answer me, you lout!

A pause.

MENDL *(To BRAYNE)* You think I'm afraid of you? What do you think you are you to me anyway? Nothing. Absolutely nothing ... Let me just ask you one little thing.

AVRUSH Don't even bother with her.

BRAYNE You pig! You drunk pig!

MENDL It's okay—I'm not afraid of her anymore. I just want to ask her one thing. One little thing. Why does she beat Reyzl. Why? A grown girl—and she beats her? Takes away her shoes? Does a *mame* do that sort of thing? If you were my *mame*, I swear—I would strangle you. Do whatever the hell you want for all I care, but just tell me one thing: Why do you beat Reyzl?!

BRAYNE Reyzl....

MENDL I'm going to tell Reyzl—I'm going to tell her that I will not let her *mame* touch her anymore. Not one finger. I won't allow it. I'll split her skull open if she does it again! I will buy her shoes ... with my own money. I'll buy them and we'll knock your teeth out. How do you like that? Just tell me: W-H-Y D-O Y-O-U B-E-A-T R-E-Y-Z-E-L?

AVRUSH Driven out of the Garden of Eden! Driven out ... My Nikhomele ... Now there's a *mentsh* for you. Her beauty, her style ...

BRAYNE You and your daughter can both drop dead for all I care.

AVRUSH The nerve! Did you hear that, Mendl? Why curse her? You witch! You aren't worth her pinky.

BRAYNE Drunk! Your own daughter refuses to see you! She's ashamed to look at your ugly face ...

AVRUSH She's afraid of you, you wild beast. She's afraid! She ... My Nikhomele is not ashamed of me. N-n-no. My Nikhomele is not ashamed ... She's afraid! She's afraid ... I'm her father after all. She's afraid of you. You are a she-devil, a beast! She is not ashamed of her *tate* ...

BRAYNE — You poor old drunk! Disgusting to even look at …

AVRUSH — Like in a dream, everything's gone. Just like a dream …

REYZL enters.

MENDL — Reyzl!

BRAYNE — What's with all this "Reyzl" suddenly? What's she to you?

REYZL — What does he want from me?

MENDL — Come here, Reyzl. Don't be afraid. Nothing's stopping you.

AVRUSH — Leave her alone! She's not your real …

BRAYNE — Mendl *Neveyle*!

MENDL — She's not your *mame*. She's not even human! She'll wind up killing you, Reyzl. Spit in her face, Reyzl! I will buy you a pair of shoes, I … Reyzl!

REYZL — What do you want from me?

BRAYNE — You piece of shit! Mendl *Neveyle*! Get out of my house *neveyle*! *(Grabbing the sack with the hide and dragging it to the door)* Get out! You and all your carcasses—get out!

MENDL snatches the sack from her.

BRAYNE — *(To AVRUSH)* You get out of here too! You and your son!

MENDL — *(Opening the sack)* I'll show you who Mendl is … *(Starts to take the hide out of the sack)* Right here in the middle of the house!

REYZL — Close the sack! I'm warning you! Close the sack!

MENDL — Reyzl—she is not your *mame*. Spit in her face! Knock out her teeth! Tomorrow, I'm buying you a pair of shoes. Expensive shoes. And then you can go wherever you want. Here's—here's some money, Reyzl!

REYZL What have I done for you …? Why are you doing this for me?

AVRUSH Driven from the Garden of Eden …

MENDL Spit in her face!

BRAYNE *(Beating REYZL)* I'm her *mame*! I'm her *mame*! I can beat her if I want! I have the right!

REYZL Save me! Please …

MENDL runs to her; a brawl ensues.

BRAYNE I'm her *mame*! I'm her *mame*! *(Laughs)*

Act Two

The same room. Several days later. Daytime. REYZL is asleep. AVRUSH enters, drunk. Notices REYZL. Goes to her and strokes her shoulder from the back.

REYZL — Who's that? What do you want?

AVRUSH — R-r-r-eyzel … You are my daughter. Aren't you, Reyzl? My d-d-daughter.

REYZL — I'm not your daughter. Go find your little Nikhomele. Go! You reek of alcohol …

AVRUSH — N-n-o, n-n-o … Nikhomele is my daughter … She … She … won't see me. Nikhomele … She's ashamed of me. You—you be my daughter. Be my daughter, please …

REYZL — God in heaven! What are you doing?!

AVRUSH — Well … I'm going to call you Nikhomele. You'll be Nikhomele. Sir, Sir, Avrush! What's become of you, Avrush? What? What? Everyone still remembers you … Everyone knew you as Sir.

REYZL — Who told you to become a drunk? Couldn't you have been like everyone else?

AVRUSH — Your *mame* … To hell! A wild beast! A banshee! Why do you stay here … In her house … Eating her food …

Food! Get a job as a maid. Be my daughter ... Please. Oh God. I shouldn't talk. I shouldn't talk ...

REYZL Why did you marry my *mame* anyway? What do you need her for? Shpriyntze divorced you, didn't she? Now Nikhomele won't see you. She's ashamed of you, yes? She's ashamed to even greet you in public ...

AVRUSH C-c-come here. Please ... *(Attempting to embrace her)*

REYZL *(Pushing him away)* Such a disgrace. An old man crying. Go lie down. Sleep it off. She'll be back soon and she'll lick your wounds.

AVRUSH I never cried when I was young ... Never. *(Walks backwards until he falls onto the bed, lies there motionless)*

There is a silence. We hear AVRUSH snoring. REYZL takes out from under her pillow a new pair of shoes and plays with them. On her face we see a childlike joy. She puts on the shoes and walks coquettishly around the room. Picks up her ripped skirt and dances around the room. MENDL enters. REYZL tries to hide her new shoes from him. A few moments of silence. They don't look at each other.

REYZL Have you seen my *mame*?

MENDL Miss her?

REYZL Your father came home stinking drunk ...

MENDL Was the Pig here?

REYZL What pig?

MENDL Don't you know who the Pig is?

REYZL I have no clue what you're talking about.

MENDL Berl *Khazer*!

REYZL And if he was here—what's it to you? That's his business! Not yours ...

MENDL Can't I even ask?

REYZL Why are you asking?

MENDL stares at her.

REYZL What are you staring at? What's with you today?

MENDL Your *mame* is vicious …

REYZL Yes? And?

MENDL I feel sorry for you is all …

REYZL I don't need your pity.

MENDL Oh really? That so? Do you even know who I am?

REYZL Your father came home stinking drunk!

MENDL If I had a *mame* like that …

REYZL Do you see your *mame* everyday?

MENDL … No.

REYZL Why?

MENDL Sometimes I see her everyday.

REYZL And Nikhomele?

MENDL Nikhomele …

REYZL You spend a lot time with her?

MENDL Who?

REYZL Nikhomele!

MENDL She—she's graduating soon.

REYZL She's your sister. Why is she ashamed to be seen in public with you?

MENDL She's ashamed?

REYZL Disgraced.

MENDL She should be ashamed … of me.

REYZL *(Showing MENDL her foot)* See?

MENDL New shoes?

REYZL You see them, don't you?

MENDL Where did you get them?

REYZL I bought them.

MENDL Who gave you the money?

REYZL I have money!

MENDL Has your *mame* seen them?

REYZL No.

MENDL There's gonna be another fight …

REYZL Let her just try and touch me … I'll knock all her teeth out. All in one swing. I'm not a child anymore.

MENDL Hah! Why should you be afraid of her? Reyzl! Do you want me on your side? Do you?

REYZL She can scream till the cows come home for all I care. I'll never go out in those stupid things again … *(Beat)* Mendl!

MENDL What?

REYZL Do you think I'm pretty? *(MENDL does not respond)* Well?

MENDL So you're not going to go out in those things anymore?

REYZL I will not. And I won't become a maid either. I'll get a job in a factory. I'll … *(Beat)* Mendl!

MENDL What do you want from me?

REYZL I asked you a question.

MENDL You're joking, right? Tell me you're joking …

REYZL Well … Tell me, Mendl. Please.

MENDL You won't be angry?

REYZL — Why would I be angry?

MENDL — The truth.

REYZL — About what?

MENDL — You swear you won't be angry?

REYZL — I already told you.

MENDL — We are not … close. We're not really friends. We're more like strangers, you and me. Not sister and brother … Just strangers.

REYZL — Look at my feet. How dainty they are in my new shoes. Dainty, right? *(MENDL does not respond)* Know who bought me these shoes?

MENDL — Who?

REYZL — You won't tell anyone?

MENDL — Why should I?

REYZL — Swear!

MENDL — I swear.

REYZL — Berl bought them.

MENDL — Berl *Khazer*?!

REYZL — Berl *Khazer*. He's a real gentleman. He brought me new shoes today … And look. Ta-da! Like a real young lady!

MENDL — How did he even know you needed shoes?

REYZL — He knew …

MENDL — Reyzl … Tell me. Why should you suffer like this? A complete stranger had to buy you a pair of shoes … Your mother is going to kill you. You know Mendl's a good soul. Listen to me, Reyzl! Do you want me to pay Berl for the shoes?

REYZL — Why?

MENDL — I want you to know that Mendl isn't who you think he is …

REYZL Mendl … Tell me. Please. I'm pretty—right? Right? Someone might even fall in love with me? Right? Mendl!

MENDL Your dress is ripped.

REYZL I'll get a new dress …

MENDL Why are you so happy?

REYZL Nobody should be sad. I'll tickle your father. Have you ever thought of asking yourself why you're so sad? Why am I so happy? No one should be sad! (MENDL tries to grab her.) Mendl! Mendele! Please—don't.

MENDL Why run away? You're always running away from me …

REYZL Me?

MENDL Why run? Do you hate me? I'm Mendl. So? We live under the same roof, we live … You know? I swear, you know … Why do you run away? Don't you remember just last night, when your *mame* was beating you? I am telling you, Reyzele—you're bad. You don't remember anything. Always forgetting. Everything! I wanted to split open her skull, I really did. I could have crushed her with one hand! I restrained myself because she's your *mame* …

REYZL What do you want me to say?

MENDL I just wanted you to know.

REYZL Why tell me this now?

MENDL Mendl isn't as bad as you think. You think I'm Berl *Khazer*? I'll speak to your *mame* if that's what you want. Say the word and she won't ever dare lift a finger to you again, Reyzl.

REYZL If you want to be nice to me … find a job for me in a factory. I want to work like all the other girls.

MENDL — I'll find one. For you, I will. You know, Reyzl … *(As he approaches her, REYZL moves away from him)* See? See.! Why do you always run away from me? Am I such an awful person that you …

REYZL — You stink. You smell like animal hides … Like dead horses. And I am clean. I bathe. Your business is with dead horses. With carcasses, with *neveyles.* I can't stand that … I wouldn't eat from the same spoon as you!

MENDL — What is it that you think I do? I sell hides … Why don't you just take an ax and split my head open, Reyzl?

REYZL — Why should I do that?

MENDL — Who told you what I do?

REYZL — You think I don't know that you skin dead horses? I like people with clean, white hands. That smell of perfume … I know I'm poor. My mother beats me … But it doesn't matter. It won't always be this way.

MENDL — Berl *Khazer* also skins horses! He does!

REYZL — That's a lie!

MENDL — I swear to you Reyzl!

REYZL — You are a liar! Berl doesn't smell. Berl is … an aristocrat. I'll tell Berl. I'll ask him if it's true …

MENDL — Here—take this stick. Take this stick and split my head open. Do it! If you're going to treat me this way, just do it! *(No reply)* Am I that bad? Tell me! Please!

REYZL — Why are you so upset?

MENDL — I … I …

REYZL — My *mame* beats me. She doesn't give me anything to eat. But who cares?

MENDL — I'm going to beat her silly! Remember last night? Listen Reyzl. Listen to me. Go outside. Just for a minute. Just go outside. You'll see for yourself … *(Smells himself)*

What do I smell like to you? Tell me! That Pig! He can drop dead for all I care. He's the one who turned you against me!

REYZL I have a nose …

MENDL I'm putting on my best clothes. I'll scrape myself clean. I'll throw the … I will. I'll find other work. I'll serve you, hand and foot. I'll treat you like a queen. Hear me? Reyzl?

REYZL is distracted by her new shoes. AVRUSH suddenly wakes up again.

AVRUSH Mendl?

REYZL Your distinguished father. The drunk!

REYZL exits.

MENDL *Tate*! *Tate*!

AVRUSH *(Speaks with difficulty)* What d'you want?

MENDL Why are you a drunk? Why … You're an embarrassment to me! Avrush! You hear me, Avrush? I don't want to be your son! Why are you always drunk-!? …

AVRUSH M-m-mendl! Your *tate* … You're going to beat your *tate*. Your old *tate* …

MENDL You're just Avrush! Nothing but a drunk … My *mame* even threw you out! Nikhomele.…

AVRUSH M-m-mendl?

MENDL Why turn me into a tanner, Avrush? Tell me … I'm curious. Everybody avoids me now. Why turn me into a *neveyle*?! I could have been a tailor. I would have been a great tailor! *(Smells his clothes)* But look at what you did to me. Why make me a *neveyle*?

AVRUSH Sir! Mendl—yes, I am a drunk. Nothing but a lousy drunk. Herds of horses. Generals rode them!

MENDL You … I could have been a tailor. I could have learned to write. I could have done that. Why turn me into a *neveyle*?

AVRUSH It's my fault, Mendl? My … my fault? Then take a stick, Mendl. Beat me. Come on! A drunk, Mendl! Beat your drunk old man! Your *mame.* Shpriyntze! It's her fault. You hear me, Mendl? She … Shpriyntze … *(Energy wanes)* Did you sell the hide? Give me some money for a drink.

MENDL I won't give you shit!

NIKHOME appears in the doorway dressed like a school girl. She is frightened.

NIKHOME Mendl, Mendl … *Mame* is sick. She wants to see you. *(Beat)* Why are you just standing there? *Mame*'s not well!

MENDL I'm coming …

AVRUSH Nikhomele … My daughter. *(Approaching her)* Nikhomele …

NIKHOME Come quickly.

NIKHOME exits.

AVRUSH *(Staggers to the door)* N-N-ikhomele! My own daughter … Tell me … Why? Tell me … Tell me why? Why?

Act Three

Shpintze's home. It is furnished very simply but tastefully and everything is very orderly. Shpriyntze lies in a bed next to a table covered with bottles of medicine Giytl sits near her. Afternoon.

SHPRIYNTZE That's the way it is, my friend. As long as you're healthy, everything's fine and dandy. Old age plays its tricks. Then, all of a sudden—BAM! It's upon you. *(Silence)* Thirty years, I've been as lonely as the night. Thirty years!

GIYTL When God smiles on you, oh! Life is one big party. But if he frowns ... You're finished.

SHPRIYNTZE I'd love to live just a little longer. Just a little longer. Nikhomele is still a child. Who knows what could happen to her? For her—I want to keep on going. But what a crazy world, my friend! People talked when I made him divorce me. But what was I supposed to do? Tell me—what? I wanted to save my little girl. That man staggers through the streets drunk.

GIYTL What was he like before?

SHPRIYNTZE Before the divorce?

GIYTL Yes.

SHPRIYNTZE Right after the wedding, I lost interest. Poof. All I can say is ... Thank goodness Nikhomele doesn't take after him. But our son! Our son's another story. He's exactly like him.

GIYTL Is he, God forbid … a drunk?

SHPRIYNTZE He lives with his father. I sent Nikhomele to get him. A *mame*'s heart aches … An only son, the only one who can say *kaddish* for me. He's my *kaddish* and I haven't seen him for probably half a year now! And Nikhomele didn't even want to go. I just barely convinced her …

GIYTL Nikhomele's a fine child, *kiyne hore.*

SHPRIYNTZE Got remarried a year ago. She has a grown daughter.

GIYTL If she married him, she's probably no better than he is!

SHPRIYNTZE What's taking her so long? Whenever she leaves the house, every minute feels like an hour! Poor thing … She really didn't want to go. *(Wincing)* Ow! I have stabbing pains all over.

GIYTL You should try mustard plaster.

SHPRIYNTZE When I'm feeling well, I'm preoccupied with my business. Nothing ever bothers me. But the second I'm lying in bed, I can't help but start thinking … Never thought about having more children. But now … Well. I think it would be easier for me if I had more children. All night, I harped on this. Finally decided to send for him. I want to see him, even though he won't be bringing me much satisfaction …

GIYTL A son is a son after all. What does he do?

SHPRIYNTZE *(Whispers)* I hear he deals with hides.

GIYTL Not a … bad business.

SHPRIYNTZE Not a bad business at all. But what good is it when he's not a *mentsh*?

GIYTL It's God's plan.

NIKHOME enters.

NIKHOME You sent me on quite an errand, *Mame* …

SHPRIYNTZE Did you go?

NIKHOME I went.

SHPRIYNTZE Were you running? You're out of breath. You're sweating!

GIYTL Now you'll have a better appetite. You should do whatever your *mame* asks. Especially a sick *mame*! What don't *mames* do for their children? That's what I want to know. Everything! They sacrifice their bodies and their souls for their children.

SHPRIYNTZE Rushing off already?

GIYTL If you only knew. I left a house full of children. Next time I come over, I'll come in the evening … Here's to a speedy recovery. Have a good day.

GIYTL exits.

NIKHOME A really fine errand you send me on …

GIYTL pokes her head back in.

GIYTL Don't forget! Mustard plaster. The best medicine …

SHPRIYNTZE Tonight, I'll do it.

GIYTL Definitely, definitely.

GIYTL exits.

SHPRINTZ What's the matter, darling?

NIKHOME You don't want to know.

SHPRIYNTZE Did you see him? Is he coming?

NIKHOME I'm not sure.

SHPRIYNTZE Was he home?

NIKHOME Yes.

SHPRIYNTZE Who else was there?

NIKHOME They were both there.

SHPRIYNTZE He was there too?

NIKHOME Yes.

SHPRIYNTZE Did anything happen?

NIKHOME No.

SHPRIYNTZE Then why are you so upset?

NIKHOME Anyone would be upset! To have a father like that! A brother like that! They live in a grave-pit. Dark—up to your neck in filth! I got as far as the porch and heard them arguing inside … I recognized Mendl's voice right away. I was afraid to open the door, I thought they might attack me.

SHPRIYNTZE Oh God …

NIKHOME I open the door. My hands are trembling … He's there drunk. He can barely stand up, mumbling. Mendl's standing next to him, grabbing him by the lapels. Shaking him.

SHPRIYNTZE He hit him? His own *tate*!

NIKHOME I don't know … I took one step inside and I couldn't go any further. They froze like statues. Stared at me like madmen. Totally insane.

SHPRIYNTZE What did you say?

NIKHOME I told Mendl you're sick and you wanted to see him.

SHPRIYNTZE And what did he say?

NIKHOME I don't know. I left right away. I thought I'd entered a den of thieves. Or a nut-house.

SHPRIYNTZE Now you know. When you were small, you used to ask: Where is my *tate*? And I'd never reply. I didn't know what to say. Now you're grown—now you understand.

You don't need me to explain it. *(After a short pause)* How does he look?

NIKHOME Who?

SHPRIYNTZE Your *tate.*

NIKHOME Dreadful. Dirty—disgusting.

SHPRIYNTZE And Mendl?

NIKHOME I thought he was crazy. A wreck. Wild hair. A monster!

SHRPINTZE What could I have done? There was no other way. He didn't want to stay with me. The devil drew him to the horses. Who does he take after? Who? What a shame. We don't have crass young men in my family. What a shame …

NIKHOME Oh, I forgot … When I was leaving, he ran after me and shouted: Nikhomele, Nikhomele! I was afraid to stay another minute.

SHPRIYNTZE You shouldn't have left. You should have talked to him. Listened to him. Maybe he had something to say …

NIKHOME I was afraid.

SHPRIYNTZE God protect us!

NIKHOME If I had a normal *tate*, a *mentsh*—maybe things would've been different. I'm so ashamed I'd rather die!

SHPRIYNTZE What can I do? I've become an invalid … What good are you when you get old? But he's my child … Your brother! I carried both of you in my belly. Both of you nursed from the same breast.

NIKHOME He's not a brother to me. I don't want to know him! I don't want to see him! When he comes—I'm leaving.

SHPRIYNTZE Don't do that, my darling. Don't. Talk to him. You only have one brother … Please, Nikhomele?

NIKHOME I'd rather have no brother.

SHPRIYNTZE — If you hadn't been so cold to him maybe he would've visited. Maybe he wouldn't have become such a stranger to his own family!

NIKHOME — But I don't want to know him! He's an idiot. For God's sake—he's a tanner!

SHPRIYNTZE lies down.

NIKHOME — Time to take your medicine *Mame.*

SHPRIYNTZE — I beg you—please, sweetheart. When Mendl comes, don't leave ...

MENDL opens the door, pokes his head in hesitantly.

SHPRIYNTZE — Come in! Come in! Why are you just standing there? Make yourself at home ... *(To NIKHOME)* Listen to me, darling. Remember what I told you ...

MENDL enters and approaches the bed.

MENDL — Are you sick, *Mame*?

SHPRIYNTZE — As you can see—I'm not well.

NIKHOME sits with her back to him paging through a book.

SHPRIYNTZE — Take a chair, sit down. Don't just stand there ...

MENDL looks around the house and then at NIKHOME

MENDL — How are you?

SHPRIYNTZE — Why don't you answer him? He's asking you how you are, Nikhomele!

NIKHOME — He can see I'm fine.

SHPRIYNTZE Why don't you sit down? Are you afraid of us?

NIKHOME brings MENDL a chair.

MENDL I'm not afraid. Why should I be afraid? What hurts you, *Mame*?

SHPRIYNTZE Those clothes you're wearing ... Look at you! Don't you have any other clothes?

MENDL My clothes?

NIKHOME Of course he doesn't have any other clothes ...

MENDL How would you know? As if she knows what's in my wardrobe! I have other clothes ...

NIKHOME Maybe you do.

SHPRIYNTZE Do you make enough to support yourself?

MENDL I make a living. What makes you think I don't?

SHPRIYNTZE Why are you so upset? Tell me, dear ... Why have you drifted away from us? It's been over six months since I last saw you. You didn't even know I was sick ...

MENDL To hell with him! He never ...

NIKHOME Don't raise your voice!

SHPRIYNTZE Always with your horses. I couldn't stand it ... I just wanted you to be successful. *A shtikl mentsh*! Look at her! Born to the same parents ... You both nursed from the same breast ... Tell me: why have you been so distant from us?

MENDL *Mame*. Why talk about this now?

SHPRIYNTZE What else should I be talking about? If I saw you more often, maybe I'd have more to talk about! *(Silence)* Where's that smell coming from you? ... Why didn't you change your clothes? Cleaner clothes.

MENDL *Mame*! What is this? I'd rather you said nothing than—

NIKHOME Don't shout at her! You can see *Mame*'s not well.

SHPRIYNTZE What did I say!? I'm just asking why you're dressed like that … You live with your father, the drunk. Who knows what kind of woman he married … What's that girl doing there anyway?

MENDL You want to know what kind of woman he married? She beats everyone. Her daughter. Even him …

SHPRIYNTZE What was she telling me? She opens the door and there you two were! Fighting with your own father!

MENDL What? Why do you look at me like that?

SHPRIYNTZE I'm your *mame*. Behave badly, fine. Choose not to live the life I had in mind for you. All the same—I can't wash my hands of you. You're still my son and I—I am your *mame*. Why are you so filthy?!

MENDL searches in his pockets.

SHPRIYNTZE What are you looking for?

MENDL I want to give you some money. I earn enough.

SHPRIYNTZE Keep your money. Keep it!

MENDL But I have money …

SHPRIYNTZE I'd rather you buy new clothes! Look at you! It's a disgrace!

NIKHOME He must like it that way.

SHPRIYNTZE Awful. Just awful!

MENDL Why are you saying this to me?!

NIKHOME Sh!

MENDL Who do you think you are? Some sister you are! To hell with you!

NIKHOME You have no right to make a scene in our home! *Mame* is not well.

MENDL Do you know this creature? I'll beat you to a pulp. You won't even know what hit you.

SHPRIYNTZE *(To NIKHOME)* Go back. Please … *(MENDL stands up)* Where are you going? Why are you so angry Mendl? What did I say? I'm your *mame*—a *mame* tells the truth … Who can say these things if not your own *mame*? Just because I said something …

MENDL *Mame*! Listen to me, *Mame*!

SHPRIYNTZE You came to visit your *mame*! Your sick *mame*!

MENDL Here I am, *Mame*! Tell me, *Mame*. Tell me why. Tell me, *Mame*—why didn't you take care of me? Why? Why did you send me away? I was just a child! Avrush—to hell with him! I'll strangle him. I'll kill him! Arvush! You'll see! Tonight—I'll strangle him. Tonight!

SHPRIYNTZE Mendl … Calm down.

NIKHOME Why don't you just leave? I told you—we shouldn't have asked him to come. Just leave!

MENDL Nasty bitch! A sister? This is a sister? *Paskude! A beyze yor af diyr*! She graduated. Such a big shot now, she thinks she's so …! You don't impress me, sis. Watch me beat you to a pulp. All of you! Tell her to shut up, *Mame*. Tell her! I'm older than you, I earn more than you …

MENDL goes toward the door.

SHPRIYNTZE Mendl … Mendl … Nikhomele! I told you not to say anything!

NIKHOME I went to summon him, this precious jewel …

MENDL Will you ever shut up?! Get away from me! I'm warning you … If you know what's good for you. I'm going to kill Avrush. Damn you … Damn all of you!

NIKHOME Get out of here! Go!

MENDL — What have they done to me?! What have they done to me! What am I? *Mame*! Tell me—what am I? *Mame*! Tell me—why are you my *mame*?!

NIKHOME tries to quiet him.

SHPRIYNTZE — Mendl … Mendl … What did I say? I didn't say anything. I just—I just asked you what that smell was. Should I not have asked?

MENDL — I stink … I stink of carcasses! I skin *neveyle*s! *Mame*! Shit! Shit! To hell with you! I hope you die a painful death!

NIKHOME — Get out! Get out! You animal!

MENDL — Go to hell! You and Reyzl can go to hell!

NIKHOME — Get out!

SHPRIYNTZE — Children! What are you doing!?

MENDL slaps NIKHOME hard. Frightens himself.

SHPRIYNTZE — The neighbors will hear … Mendl!

MENDL — I'll strangle you and Reyzl!

SHPRIYNTZE — Nikhomele, calm down! Please!

NIKHOME — He's nauseating! He's contaminated the whole house!

MENDL curls up on his mother's bed.

MENDL — What have they turned me into?

SHPRIYNTZE — Quiet, now. I didn't say anything, darling. Relax …

MENDL is silent, attentive to her voice. He gets up and looks around bleary eyed. He studies his clothes, takes the lapel of his coat, and rips it off.

MENDL *(Mumbing) Neveyle, neveyle,* Avrush, Reyzl.

Act Four

Same room as the first act. During the day. AVRUSH is lying in bed, snoring.

AVRUSH *(Waking up, he sings)* From out of dire straits—I called to God. *Miyn hameytzar korosiy ko! Miyn miyn miyn! Korosiy korosiy! Korosiy ko.* I called out to God—Avrush! … Avrush …!

AVRUSH pulls a bottle of whiskey out of his pocket and drinks. He hides the empty bottle under his pillow and lies down again. MENDL enters and locks the door. His hair is disheveled. His clothes are torn to shreds. He runs back and forth and then suddenly comes to a standstill, deep in thought.

AVRUSH *(Singing in his sleep) M-i-y-n h-a mey-tz-a-r.*

MENDL throws himself on top of AVRUSH wildly and starts to strangle him with a wild roar. AVRUSH's limbs are flailing. MENDL stretches out on top of him and continues to strangle him with all of his might, roaring unintelligible sounds. He stands up and looks around dazed. He tries to lift AVRUSH's arm then his leg. AVRUSH lies motionless. MENDL climbs off the bed and shakes AVRUSH.

MENDL Avrush! Avrush! Avrush? Huh? Avrush?! Reyzl! Reyzl! (*MENDL stands very still as if to deny what has just happened)* The meadow … In the meadow, birds are flying. In the meadow—in the meadow, horses are leaping. In the meadow—in the meadow, geese! Geese, everywhere! *(He stands for a moment deep in thought, then starts looking about and shouting)* Reyzl? Reyzl! Reyzl! *(He looks under the bed, under the trunks. Approaches AVRUSH and looks under him)* Reyzl? Reyzl! Reyzl! Come out. Please—come out. I promise, I won't let your *mame* beat you. I swear! It's ok to come out. Your *mame* is not here. Come out! *(Singing) Afn lonke, afn lonke, ferdlach shrpingen afn lonke, afn lonke, feglach fliehen. (He smells his clothes)* Poot-poot-poot! Avrush, Avrush! Reyzl, come here. Come to me, quickly. Quickly! Look at what a handsome bridegroom I am!! Come here! (*He pulls his trunk out from under the bed and tries to open it, but it is locked. He tries to force it open)* Open up! *(He kicks it. He finds an ax in the corner and tries to open the trunk with it. Then he suddenly approaches Avrush.) Tate*! *Tate*! Wake up! *(Laughs)* Wake up, *Tate*! Wake up, Avrush! Lots of horses … I've brought horses. Horses! *(Singing) Afn lonke afn lonke ferdlech ferdlech. (Tries once again to open the trunk.)* Eh eh eh! There's Reyzl! *(Laughs and puts his ear to the hole in the lock on the trunk)* Are you in there? Huh? In there? Open up! Open up! Look I have lots of money to give you. Lots of money! *(Takes his wallet out of his pocket and spills the money onto the top of the truck. He knocks on the trunk with the coins)* Listen, Reyzl! I'm giving you money. Come out! Open up! Open up! Open up or you'll be sorry. *(He picks up the coins he spilled onto the trunk and puts themin his pocket. He jumps on top of the trunk. Laughs. Climbs back down and hacks the lid with the ax, ripping a hole into it. He peers into the trunk)* Well are you coming out? *(He takes the things out of the trunk one by one, and inspects everything carefully and puts them aside. Little by little he empties the entire trunk. Looks through the clothes)* Reyzl … Where are you? Tell me! *(Cries)* Where are you? Come. *(He turns over the trunk, shakes it and looks to see if anything has fallen out. He stands in the same spot and looks around hopelessly. He begins to run around the room. Stops next to AVRUSH's bed and stares at him. Suddenly leaves the bedside and shouts as if he's the sexton announcing the Sabbath [Shabbos].)* Everybody get to *shul*! *(He looks at his clothes and notices that they are ripped. With amazing speed he begins to rip strips from his top coat. He rips every strip into the smallest pieces possible. He smells each piece and throws each piece away with disgust. He takes his Shabbos clothes and dusts them off. After smelling his Shabbos shoes a few times, he dusts them off. He puts the Shabbos clothes on over the rags he is wearing. Takes his Shabbos hat from the wall and puts it on. Everything is done with amazing speed. With unusual purpose. He puts the remaining things back into the trunk and puts it under the bed. He tidies up. He smells his hands. Finds a knife and starts to peel away at the skin on his hands. He finds a mirror, looks in it, throws it to the ground and runs off-stage.)*

REYZL and BERL enter.

BERL — That piece of shit Mendl *Neveyle*'s not here. I swear I'll take his head off. Is Avrush sleeping? Some shoes! Baby Doll! You are a Baby Doll! *(Pulls her close)* What did Mendl *Neveyle* say?

REYZL — Things. But I don't believe him. He said them out of anger, just anger.

BERL — Tell me what you're afraid of then.

REYZL — It doesn't matter what he said. I swear—

BERL — Tell me. You'll be sorry if you don't …

REYZL — So stubborn, Berl.

BERL You'll be sorry, Reyzele.

REYZL What if I don't want to tell you?

BERL Then I won't say another word. Berl doesn't like to make trouble.

REYZL He said you skin dead horses too.

BERL What? Where is he?! I'll break every bone in his body! *(Laughs)* And you believed him?

REYZL I told you—I didn't believe him. Actually—I told him I thought he was lying. I told him you smell like an aristocrat …

BERL No matter. I told you, Baby Doll … Berl is the best. You'll see. Reyzl, I'll buy you a diamond ring. A diamond ring!

REYZL My *mame*. She'll tear my hair out.

BERL I'll come back. Later. No … I'll wait until she comes home. Confront her. I'll grab her by the collar and I'll say: "Listen Brayne, Braynele! If you just try to lift a finger to Reyzl one more time, there'll be nothing left of you to bury!" And you, Reyzl. Just watch. Don't say a word. Just watch, okay? *(Beat)* Well? No? Tell me!

REYZL But she's my *mame* …

BERL A *mame* like that? You should spit in her face! "Reyzl is mine." That's what I'll tell her. Berl will show you.

REYZL I'm yours?

BERL So you were talking to that stinking animal. What else did he tell you? Listen, Reyzl. First, I'll tear him apart. You understand? Then—Reyzl? Reyzele! I am Berl *Khazer*. You better know what that means. You better not be messing with me … Are you? I am Berl the Pig!

REYZL Are you threatening me? Why?

BERL Reyzele …

REYZL — You talk about beating up my *mame*—but I don't want you to. Please. *(Sweetening)* Berele … Come on. Come. Let's dance. Let's dance until my *mame* gets home.

BERL — Answer my question.

REYZL — What?

BERL — You want that diamond ring?

REYZL — Buy me a dress first. If you want to be my treasure—that's the way to my heart. Look at this ripped rag. It's even shabbier next to these new shoes …

BERL — What then?

REYZL — Then I'll have new shoes and a new dress.

BERL — Don't play with me. Playing with Berl is like playing with fire.

REYZL — I'm pretty, yes? *(BERL does not answer. He is transfixed as REYZL sings) Afn heykhn barg, afn griyne groz, ziytzen panes tzvey. Sheyne bochrim mit diy frakn kumen dort tzu zey, kumen dort tzu zey!* On the hilltop, on the green grass, sit two ladies. Well-dressed boys are meeting them there, meeting them there.

BERL — What's that song? Reyzl?

REYZL — *(Singing) Un die panes lieben zey, un die panes* … And the ladies love them, and the ladies …

BERL — Why sing a song like that?

REYZL — Don't you hear the words? Listen! There on the hilltop in the grass near the forest sit beautiful ladies and to the ladies come suitors and they love them—and that's all.

BERL — Reyzl, Reyzl! Tell me …

REYZL — Berl … *(Sweetening)* You tell Mendl that he shouldn't dare speak to me.

BERL — Don't you worry. Count on it. I'll give him a talking to that he's going to remember for the rest of his life.

REYZL I can't look at him. I spit on him. He's a stinking animal. I'm not kidding, Berl ... He asked me to marry him! *(Laughs)* Berl, baby ... Tell him not to touch me. Please.

BERL You just leave it all to me. I'll pay him back. For everything. I'll show him who skins animals. Reyzl! You hear me? For the last time—listen. This is the last time I'm going to say it. Remember who you're playing with here.

REYZL *(Embracing him)* Do you love me that much?

BERL kisses her.

BERL Tell me the truth. When I say—and listen to me, now, listen hard—when Berl says something ... that's all it takes.

BRAYNE enters carrying two baskets of fish. Gives REYZL a sharp look. Puts down the baskets and sits down exhausted.

REYZL What's wrong, *Mame*?

BRAYNE Get away from me, you ... you slut!

REYZL It was just a question!

BRAYNE Get away from me! I'll split your head open in a minute ... I work myself to death and she's home screwing around ... I can't take care of you anymore. What—what are those? Shoes? New shoes?! Where did you get those? Take them off! Right now. This very minute! *(She grabs something to hit REYZL with)* Take them off, you slut!

BERL Brayne, stop this! You hear me? Berl *Khazer* is talking to you! Just try and disobey me.

BRAYNE Who in the hell do you think you are? Telling me? What to do ... with my own daughter? *Khazer*! Swine!

BERL — I'll only tell you once more. Shut your trap! Brayne! I'm ordering you! If you don't, I'll go ahead and shut it for you.

REYZL — Berl! Berl—stop!

BERL — Reyzl is mine! You understand? You don't own her! She's mine!

BRAYNE — Reyzl is yours? Yours?! Pig! *(Slaps REYZL)* Reyzl's mine! She's mine! My daughter! My daughter! *(Gives her another slap)* I am her *mame*!

BERL — Get away from me!

BRAYNE — *(To AVRUSH) Gevald*! He's going to kill me! Abba! Abba! Avrush—you bum! Wake up! Get up! Call the police. Avrush! Avrush—you deadbeat! Get up. Get the police! *(She realizes he is dead) Shema Yisroyl*! Avrush! Oh! Oh, Abba! Abba! He's … dead! He must've passed out. Call … Call someone. Quick! Call someone! Please!

BERL — *(Tries to wake AVRUSH)* Abba! Abba! He's out cold! Get some water.

MENDL — *(From offstage) Afn lonke afn lonke feyglech fliehen …*

MENDL enters with blood running down his face, trembling from the cold. His clothes are torn. He smiles at everyone. From offstage we hear CHILDRENS' VOICES shouting: "He's in the basement. He's in the basement!" MENDL is grimacing bizarrely, sniffing the air and saying: "Poot poot!". He sniffs his hands and starts to tear the skin off his fingers. Blood drips from his fingers.

REYZL — Help! Help! He's gone mad.

MENDL — *(Walks slowly to AVRUSH's bed and sings)* Mendl *Neveyle* … Avrush … Mendl *Neveyle … afn lonke, afn lonke …*

CURTAIN

Dammerung or Twilight (Tzvishn Tog un Nakht)

By Peretz Hirshbein

Translated from Yiddish by Mark Altman and Ellen Perecman

Adapted by Mark Altman, Ellen Perecman, Clay McLeod Chapman, Dana Zeller-Alexis and Mark Zeller

Characters

NOSN	*Zeyde* (Grandfather)
NODOV	Nosn's first born son
HIYMEN	Nosn's second son
TOMER	Nodov's teenaged daughter
ZIYZI	Nodov's younger daughter
YOUNG WOMAN	
OLD MAN	
YOUNG GIRL	

Act One

Morning light comes through the window of a small house in a wooded area.

ZIYZI He went straight into the forest.

NOSN What did he look like?

ZIYZI Dark skin. And he had lots of hair.

NOSN It's him. Definitely.

ZIYZI I'm going to see what Daddy's doing.

NOSN Stay. God has filled your father's heart with sorrow. Tell me where you saw the man.

ZIYZI Like I said—he went out that door. Tell me, *Zeyde*, why is Daddy always so sad? Whenever Tomer spends time with him, she comes back crying.

NOSN Because she loves him.

ZIYZI Because she loves him? I love him too! I'm the one who's going to see him. I'll sing and dance for him. I'll sing like the birds in the forest. That'll make him happy.—Let's go, *Zeyde*?

NOSN is lost in thought.

ZIYZI Why are you so sad, *Zeyde*?

NOSN My beard is turning gray.

ZIYZI I'll pluck out the gray and you'll be as young as Daddy. *(Hugs him) Zeyde*! *Zeyde*! I love you so much! Will you take me with you wherever you go?

NOSN As long as you want to come along.

ZIYZI If we go far, you'll have to carry me … No, you won't have to carry me … You won't have to carry me. Look how far we went today and I didn't get tired.

NOSN *(To himself)* Today the sun is still beautiful, radiant. And tomorrow—who knows?

ZIYZI It'll be beautiful again. The sun rises every day.

NOSN It's as though you were born in the forest and grew up in the trees.

ZIYZI *(Laughs)* As though I grew up in the trees! Watch—I can imitate a cuckoo: Kookookoo! Here's how a crow sounds: kra kra!

NOSN That's enough, my child. Enough.

ZIYZI I can imitate all the birds. *(She imitates various bird calls)*

NOSN Quiet. One mustn't sing like a bird now. A winged-thief is in our midst.

ZIYZI Can he fly into our house? No. You're just saying that so I won't sing, aren't you? I know you don't like my singing …

TOMER enters wearing a white dress. She has been crying.

TOMER *Zeyde*! Where were you? Have you heard anything?

NOSN Speak quietly, my child. Not so loud … Why all this crying?

TOMER I'll cry so much, my tears will dissolve the earth.

NOSN — Did you see anyone pass by our house? Someone of middle-age?

TOMER — I don't think there is anyone left on earth. Everyone's drained the life out of everyone else.

NOSN — Stay inside. There's thunder and lightning. Everything is shivering with fear. Everything in the world. The very heavens are descending upon the earth.

TOMER — Father is so sad. *Zeyde*, who planted this cruelty in humankind? …

NOSN — How would I know? Night dwells in my heart. Awaiting its final hour. Whatever happens, I've considered everything. I've prepared for anything …

TOMER — *Zeyde* … Talk to me of mercy. Of love. Burning tears. Talk to me of a beautiful, bright dawn, when the deadly terror that hangs over this earth will disappear.

NOSN — I will tell you what it was like when your father was a very young child. My wife bore two, two sons …

ZIYZI — I want to sit next to *Zeyde*.

TOMER — How can we reawaken people's generosity toward one another? How can we restore goodness and tenderness in people? *Zeyde*, when you were young, were things as they are now?

NOSN — Everything is as it was. The same sinfulness in man's heart, the same … Only the punishment differs. God doesn't offer the same punishment.

TOMER — Is that why people are as vicious as wild animals? I'm just waiting for my father to command me … I will spread my arms wide, I will go amidst the people, I will call out with all my strength: "Have mercy on one another, my brothers and sisters". They need only be reminded. I am prepared to die for them.

NOSN — There was a time when people were extraordinarily sinful. The Earth itself—this beloved, good Earth—could no longer bear the weight of their sins. God brought a flood upon them. Not even a memory remained of what had been on this Earth. But God regretted his actions. He swore never to send a flood again—and he said to the people. Your good deeds to one another will be your reward—and your evil deeds to one another will be your punishment ... the punishment that people will bring upon themselves is even more terrible than the flood itself. God flooded the earth with water, and the people will flood the world with their very own blood ...

TOMER — It's not true! God's punishment wouldn't be that horrible. I will awaken the mercy in people's hearts; I will make them drunk with love.

ZIYZI — *Zeyde*, tell us about the birds. About angels that fly around in the forest at night.

NOSN — But let's hear how it ends ... Shhhh ... Quiet ... Their profound self-hatred will bring blood to their eyes. Their teeth will grow sharp and long, like wolves who wander in the dark of night. They will grow talons like vultures, their hearts will become hard and dry, and thirsty for hot human blood. Men and women will roam the earth sniffing the air for the scent of blood.

TOMER — Horrifying!

NOSN — The day is near. The hour is upon us. The heavens will be draped in dark clouds. Heaven will not know what transpires on earth.

TOMER — That can't happen.

NOSN — What my cold heart feels, my mouth cannot express.

TOMER — I can hear Father.

ZIYZI — Stay with *Zeyde*, I'll go upstairs ... I'll sing my new songs for him.

TOMER — Sit in his lap; stroke his head.

ZIYZI I'll sing for him.

ZIYZI runs offstage. NOSN hears something.

TOMER What is it, *Zeyde*?

NOSN I can already hear them roaring.

TOMER It's just the wind, *Zeyde*.

NOSN Not just the wind, my child. God's voice is in the wind. His voice never frightens me.

TOMER It's the trembling of the branches. The rustling of leaves.

NOSN It's the beating of human hearts. It will only get louder. God's voice will become weaker. It will be drowned out by the wild roar.

ZIYZI's voice is heard from upstairs.

TOMER Why is Ziyzi screaming?

NOSN No, my child, she's singing. She is singing him the song of innocence. The only song left. Let her sing to him, let her sing to him. He needs to hear it. Let her sing to him—and you, listen to me. You've become such a stranger to me. What I say doesn't make sense to you any more.

TOMER *Zeyde*! My heart is full of love for you, for Father, for all humankind! Speak *Zeyde*, I am listening …

NOSN Soon I will be silent. There will be no one for me to speak to … I will wander alone in the forest, like an uprooted tree, its branches broken …

TOMER I will be there with you, *Zeyde*.

NOSN You will be torn from me.

TOMER No one will tear me away from you, from Father. My heart belongs to the whole world, my compassion is for everyone … I will wash everyone's wounds. Do you hear? Everyone's!

NOSN Your heart is pure and innocent—but you came into this world to know only punishment. And I will wander in the woods in silence …

TOMER *Zeyde* … Who is going to harm you?

NOSN My own son will pierce my heart with his nails.

TOMER My father? *Zeyde*—My father whose heart is torn with suffering, he will do this to you? I don't believe that *Zeyde*!

NOSN Your father is as gentle as a dove. That is how he came into this world. But a brother was born to him—a younger one.

TOMER Where is he?

NOSN I have never mentioned him.

TOMER Neither has Father.

NOSN Your father was afraid of him. Their mother carried them both: your warmhearted father, and years later—the other one, in the same womb. They nursed from the same breast—but God did not create both of them in the same form. Each of them peered out through entirely different eyes. Your father was born as pure as an angel. His eyes were innocent as the eyes of a dove. But his brother was as angry as a snake, from the moment he was born … His eyes were as sharp as an eagle's eyes.

TOMER Where is he now?

NOSN He disappeared when he was quite small. He grew wings. Suddenly he started to fly. He flew away. I have never forgotten him. I can never forget him. His burning eyes still linger in the cradle … This is the surest sign that he is alive. The heart can never forget a living, breathing human being. The heart never forgets.

TOMER He must have died by now. If we haven't heard from him for such a long time, surely he's dead …

NOSN He appears in my thoughts. I see him. As a grown man, almost your father's age … He is somewhere near our house … He brings misfortune with him.

TOMER What do you mean, *Zeyde*?

NOSN He will rend my heart with his talons. I will wander in the forest with a torn heart …

TOMER I will blunt the eagle's talons. I will soften his sharp looks with love.

NOSN I think someone just passed by the house.

TOMER I'll see who's there.

NOSN I hear the sound of his wings … I feel his sharp talons.

TOMER *Zeyde*, calm yourself. My heart will shield you.

ZIYZI enters.

ZIYZI There! Through the window! He's coming right toward our house.

NOSN My time has come.

HIYMEN enters.

HIYMEN You may be old and gray, bent with sorrow—but I recognize you, Father!

NOSN I knew you'd come …

HIYMEN You remember me?

NOSN I never forgot you. My heart has been uneasy. But now that you've arrived, I feel strong enough to leave this place in peace.

HIYMEN Age has not broken your pride.

NODOV enters.

NODOV It's you my brother.

HIYMEN I would have thought your bones had been carried away in my cradle by a river of blood long ago. *(Points to TOMER and ZIYZI)* These are your children? Both of them take after you.

NODOV They've grown up in difficult times. Are you going to tell me why you're here?

HIYMEN What is born on this earth must in the end find its way back to earth. I have often peered into your windows, but I didn't dare disturb you. I watched your children grow up. You no longer stand erect. Old age has caught up with our father.

TOMER I never heard anyone mention …

NOSN Age has caught up with your father. When he was born, an angel with a wry smile showed him a desert, where a solitary figure wandered, his head bowed low, and the angel said: Just as lonely and bitter will you wander among your own thoughts throughout your life.

HIYMEN I am proud to be your son. You have gone your own way your entire life, and you will choose your own path until the very end. I don't even hope to be able to take you with me.

NOSN Did you intend to take me away from here? After you were born I stopped hoping for anything. With my eyes wide open, I gave up hope. I am hopelessness itself.

HIYMEN I know that my efforts are in vain when it comes to you, Father. But the children … Perhaps my brother and I will …

NODOV … You want me to go with you? If you have found the true path, how to free yourself from the web entangling our lives, then Brother—I will go with you. Have you brought the secret of how to make people stop and look around at least for a moment—then Brother I will go with you … We will shout: "Stop people! What are you doing?" All life can lead to eternal promise. If only everyone were to hear these words.

HIYMEN You are lost my brother. Your own thoughts are leading you astray …

NODOV I remember that grin. You will remain who you are, scoffing at everything, and I will remain who I am. My heart bleeds for everyone. Your heart is as hard as steel and as sharp as a spear … My heart is always in tumult and my life under a hail of fire … Divine flames tantalize me from a distance. I can see them. I think that at any moment I will find the true path. I move on in life—I step onto the battlefield, I cry out. Everyone is silent—Everyone. From the highest to the lowest, they all hear my words … The beating of every heart ceases and my words penetrate them.

HIYMEN Why are you still in this house then?

NODOV All of a sudden the divine flames are being snuffed out and a cloud of smoke is obscuring my dreams!

TOMER What are you saying Father! Don't recant everything you have taught me.… Your words have meant so much. They move me, they awaken my soul. "With mercy, with passionate love …" This is what you taught me Father! I am ready to do as you ask …

HIYMEN You, my brother, are sending your child as a sacrifice. All that is beautiful, all that is pure, have people trampled with their calloused feet long ago. Tell me. For whose sins are you offering these sacrifices? For your own? Perhaps for the sins of your youth. Perhaps you, Father, are demanding a sacrifice to old age.

NOSN I am silent. My tongue must remain silent …

TOMER Father is not sending me. I go willingly to extinguish the fire with my own hands!

HIYMEN You will be burned … There is no return from this path you have chosen.

NODOV Can I say of my hand that it is not mine? If you cut it—my heart stops. Can I say this eye does not belong to me when what it sees awakens my thoughts? Can I say this head is not my own? Can I disavow life? I was born on the earth and I grew up on the earth. My heart is being torn, my head burns, my blood rushes … and I, with all my strength must cry "Stop! Stop!" I will cry until my tongue is torn out … Come upstairs with me. You'll see through the window how far the stream of blood has reached.

NODOV exits.

HIYMEN I will show my brother that he has been peering through the same small window his entire life …

HIYMEN follows NODOV out. TOMER is deep in thought.

NOSN When eagles descend upon the earth—people must hide in the forests.

NOSN exits.

ZIYZI *Zeyde*, I'm coming.

ZIYZI exits dancing.

Act Two

At the foot of a hill just outside the forest. Purple red from the sunset.

NOSN — Death is still miles away. Already I have been driven into the forest. Tomer is being pulled in opposite directions, as by two magnets. And Ziyzi is so young that she can still get lost in the tall grass. (*ZIYZI appears)* Ziyzi! Ziyzi! (*ZIYZI runs toward him)* She is still so young and innocent.

ZIYZI — *Zeyde*! *Zeyde*!

NOSN — Don't shout, don't shout, my child.

ZIYZI — Where have you been *Zeyde*? I missed you. I looked for you everywhere, among the trees.

NOSN — I love you, my child, you missed …

ZIYZI — Why did you leave, *Zeyde*?

NOSN — It's better in the forest. It's more peaceful in the forest … Did you see your father, my child?

ZIYZI — I'll go get him. Ok, *Zeyde*? Tomer misses you too. Daddy, too. Everyone misses you. I wanted to cry.

NOSN — They miss me?!

ZIYZI — Are you afraid of him, *Zeyde*? I'm not. He's so nice. He put his arms around me and he told me a story.

NOSN What did he tell you?

ZIYZI I forgot … *Zeyde*, where does Tomer want to go … Why is Daddy sad?

NOSN My child, I will take you into the forest and you will hear the birds sing …

ZIYZI And then I'll sing like a bird.

ZIYZI sings and is playful with NOSN.

NOSN You are wild, my child. God created your body and your soul to be free. You are not of this world, of this time.

ZIYZI looks at him, picks grass and puts it on his head. NOSN doesn't notice.

NOSN A sheep goes out to pasture in the green valley.—Does she know that a wolf is sharpening his teeth there? Can she sense it … or does it come to her in a dream?

ZIYZI *Zeyde*, are you talking to me?

NOSN To you … to myself … to the forest, to the trees, to the earth … A child sleeps peacefully. Does the child know that the city is under siege? That the spear is being sharpened? The trees stand upright and point with pride toward the sky … I hear the sharpening of the saw. I hear the chopping of wood in a far corner of the forest.

ZIYZI They won't chop down this forest. I promise they will not chop it down!

NOSN The dark cloud is approaching from a direction I never anticipated. But could I keep it at bay even if it were the size of my hand …?

ZIYZI *Zeyde*! I'm going, I'm going home.

NOSN — If you want to see a real sunset you cannot sit in the valley, you must not sit in the valley. I have rested my feet. Now I will try to climb a little higher. If I see the sunset clearly then I will know what the next day will bring.

The forest is covered in the purple color of the sunset.

ZIYZI — Do you mean up the hill, *Zeyde*? If I go up the hill with you, then you have to take me home …

NOSN — In the east the forest is already painted blue—it won't be long before the sun sets …

ZIYZI — Tell me, *Zeyde*, why are you so scared? I won't go with you if you are scared.

NOSN — Let's go.

ZIYZI — *Zeyde*, you be the old shepherd and I will be the white lamb; wherever you go, I will follow you. And if a wolf tries to attack me I will hide under your coat and I will cry "Meh, meh, meh."

NOSN — Come my little sheep, come. I will teach you how to protect yourself from a wolf. I will teach you how to look at the sunset and know what kind of day tomorrow will be.

NOSN exits toward the forest. ZIYZI leaps after him, calling "meh" like a young sheep. As TOMER is about to go into the forest, HIYMEN appears and blocks her path. TOMER tries to pass him.

HIYMEN — Wait. Don't rush off.

TOMER — Let me pass.

HIYMEN — Where are you going?

TOMER — Where my soul has been beckoning me for so long. The moment has arrived. Everything must happen tonight.

HIYMEN — Did your father send you?

TOMER My father's wish is also my own. But even if he has a change of heart, I will never turn back. Nothing in the world could make me turn back.

HIYMEN He is abandoning you midstream. Your wounded heart has been shaped by his weak fingers …

TOMER My father is strong. In his heart—fire contends with water. His heart reflects tragedy and pain. I am like my father, but I still have my youth … Youth and suffering like the ocean, wide and wild. My father, who suffers for everyone, is in my heart and in my thoughts. My blood rushes when I see the suffering in his face. I suffer with him … and now I must go and fall at people's feet, and beg them: "Cease your murderous war of brother against brother."

HIYMEN You will not bring a beautiful new dawn with your tears. Even if thousands of sisters join you in a river of tears it will be nothing more than a choir of misery. And for what? This obscene dance of death. I have come to save your life, because you were raised in the same nest where I spent my youth. Come with me!

TOMER *Zeyde* says disaster follows you wherever you go …

HIYMEN I had to come back. Do you understand? I yearned for this place … My heart pined like a dry autumn leaf that rips itself from the tree to rot in the bosom of the earth. Like the rays that tear themselves away from the sun's breast to reach down to the tall petals of lilies. It's longing that gives form to the most beautiful splendor beneath the heavens. Out of longing, the mighty mountain explodes, spewing forth pieces of its burning heart towards heaven, flooding the entire area with liquid fire … My heart yearned with a violence, the violence of a storm that churns the oceans and smashes ancient forests …

TOMER I hid behind the mountain and watched from a distance as a sea of sorrow lapped our mountain. People are drowning in their own blood … Struggling … Do you understand how terrifying this is? Come with me, come. Perhaps Father has also had a change of heart by now. Come with me. And if you won't, I am going alone. I'll go alone singing the eternal song of love for everyone. I will sing to them from my aching heart—let me go.

HIYMEN My child! There's a beautiful island standing alone in the middle of the wide sea … A young king sits on a throne and he longs, and he waits—for the young queen of his heart … Nature, dressed in her green robes and covered by a thin veil, yearns with the young king. He made the Desires swear that they would bring him his beloved from no matter how far … the Desires rush off, striving to overtake each other, beating each other violently without end … They can not carry out his command … At dawn he makes the moon swear before the morning star that she will bring him his beloved … with a pale, veiled face the moon set in the east.… At sunset, he makes the sun swear to find his beloved.—You see, the sun's rays are wandering among the trees. They are looking for the young queen. They are looking for you. Leave your home, young queen! Before the last ray of sunlight fades …

TOMER What a cold heart you have! Cold and angry. There is a wild fire burning in your eyes; it's frightening me. Let me go. Let me return to my father.

HIYMEN Your yearning is even more foolish than his. Your father's love has poisoned you …

TOMER Your eyes burn like an angry snake.

HIYMEN My eyes are fired by my heart and my heart is fired by the sun that reaches the peaks of the highest mountains …

TOMER Do you have any idea what is happening among the people? … Their souls are tattered. They have forgotten how to love, to have mercy. We need only remind them, come with me! Mercy and love will heal the whole world.

HIYMEN Mercy! *(Laughs)* Worms invented it ... as they lay trampled on the ground. With tears in their eyes they begged "Mercy, Mercy." The earth is in shambles. False prophets have soiled it. They have taken people's souls, souls that have always strived toward heaven,—and chained them to the earth. Come with me, and I will release you from this place so that your soul can once again be purified ...

TOMER Don't you understand that the new dawn is upon us?

HIYMEN My child, those blind, clawing moles can't bring this beautiful dawn. *(Laughs)* Worms squirm and search for beams of light from suns long exhausted—they pick up fallen stars out of the mud ... life itself will create the sun that will bring this new dawn, these hearts will ignite the sun.....

Rays of sunlight fall on TOMER.

TOMER Look how beautiful the sunset is ...

HIYMEN Rays of sunlight are searching for the young Queen. They want to protect her from the furious night that's falling.

TOMER The moon was out last night. I stole quietly away through the window to see what was going on. My father's nervous pacing had kept me awake. I went a distance from the house hoping to find the dark secret that prevents my father from closing his eyes. There was silence all around me ... I went as far as the valley beneath the forest and sat in the silence. Suddenly a light blue haze rose from the valley. It grew bigger and wider. It enveloped the entire area in a thin transparent veil. Heaven and earth appeared as one. I didn't know where I was—whether in heaven or on earth ... Suddenly I felt a gentle wind. The blue haze disappeared. I thought that I had either ascended to heaven or that heaven had descended to the earth … Flickering stars had been planted all around me as far as the eye could see. Tonight will be another and …

HIYMEN And?

TOMER You are tearing my heart with your talons. Father! … I hear you calling … I'm coming … I love you so much! … *(To HIYMEN)* Look softly into my eyes. I will tell you everything … I cannot! I cannot …

TOMER drops at HIYMEN's feet.

HIYMEN You can.

TOMER *(Speaking as if from a dream)* I was sitting in the valley. I wanted to see what I could hear in the distance. Slumber caressed my brow. … I dreamt … My eyes were open … Father sat writing and I sat quietly in the corner and looked into his eyes in the distance. How they sparkled with each new thought that ran through his head. The door opened and a snow white hand appeared. It signaled to me. I don't know whose hand it was. I had never seen such a white hand. I left the house unwittingly … and I noticed the hand again … It motioned me to go on … I kept walking … I kept walking … The hand vanished and in its place appeared a pair of burning eyes … rays emanating from them, their gaze stroking my face … They signaled me to go on. I went as far as the mountain on the other side of the forest … The eyes disappeared … I was left sitting alone … A frightful longing came over me. Where have you taken me? You are crushing my heart … let me go!

HIYMEN I want to heal your crushed heart.

TOMER Have mercy on me! Let me go to the naked, newly born chicks lying in their cradles crying for their mothers:

"*Mame!* … *Mame*! …" People are wandering aimlessly begging for love and mercy. Wandering alone without a mother or a father … An entire world of orphans. I'm coming. I am bringing you my heart exploding with love … let me go! Let me go!

A pause.

HIYMEN And what about your crushed heart?

TOMER A thick black cloud drifted over from the west. It was as if it rose from the earth.… it hovered right over our house, enveloping it.… I was overcome by fear for my father's life, and I ran home to save him … but where our house once stood I found a large black cloud—Father! Dear Father!

HIYMEN Did the cloud crush him?

TOMER No! No! My father's voice rang out from beneath the cloud as clear and strong as always: "They stoned the prophet to death but his words were carried through the air, and like burning arrows they plunged into the sinning hearts. They drove the prophet from the city into the desert, but divine flames shot from his eyes. He has remained amidst the people … the sparks are still there and people run from them their entire lives!" … His words pierced the black cloud, like flames, and they flew directly up to heaven … My father! My father!—I cried—I am your child and you are my father … send me into fire—and I will go; into water, I will go … and I threw myself into the black cloud …

HIYMEN And then you woke up?

TOMER No. I wasn't sleeping. I was dreaming about love and mercy.

HIYMEN The sun has already set. It's getting dark … people will get lost in the angry night that's falling. They won't see each other—They'll see only themselves. And instead of piercing a beloved friend's breast with their spears, they will pierce their own hearts … The night will go on and on … This moment between night and day will go on and on until the last poor soul has been annihilated … until the last person is trampled by his brother like a filthy worm … The breaking day is not more than a reflection of a distant dream … A reflection of rays from a sun that has been absent for a long time. Today, true light pours across a place that an ordinary mind dare not dream of … and when a ray of that eternal life falls on one of the thousands of newly born children … it grows eagle's wings that carry the child away from this earth …

TOMER Where?

HIYMEN To the great eagles' nest. For years, the order of the eagles has been gaining power on earth—… Not eagles that lust for corpses, or thirst for blood … eagles that will bring the true light on their wings … the light that will drive the night away and remain forever bright …! You must choose!

TOMER *(Rubs her eyes as if she has just awoken from a deep sleep)* I'm late. They're waiting for my love.

TOMER exits.

HIYMEN I have to save her life …

HIYMEN follows TOMER out. It grows dark. A church bell rings in the distance and then silence. A young woman hurries by looking about in fright. She clutches a baby to her breast protectively. She disappears. Someone else runs by as if looking for somewhere to hide. A double chime of the church bell is heard. An old man appears, walking with two canes. He quickly disappears. A young girl runs, notices a house in the distance, stops for a moment as if deciding what to do. She disappears. It grows darker. The tumultuous clanging of the church bells becomes more frequent. A wind rips through the forest and there is movement among the trees.

Act Three

A dark, windy night. From time to time lightening bolts appear. We hear the echo of distant shouting. NOSN and ZIYZI are sitting on a hill.

NOSN See how beautiful God's world is at night.

ZIYZI No *Zeyde*, this isn't beautiful. It's going to rain very hard soon. My feet hurt—I want you to take me home right now.

NOSN It's dangerous to be at home now. Stay with me. I will not let anyone steal you away ...

ZIYZI Where's Daddy, and Tomer?

NOSN I feel it in my heart. Everything will happen tonight.

ZIYZI Why are we walking in the field?

NOSN Are you homesick?

ZIYZI Yes. Why did you leave our home and take me with you?

NOSN I want you to get used to being away from home so that you feel at home in the forest.

ZIYZI Will we live here like birds?

NOSN We will live here like all God's creatures. Come.

ZIYZI Will we grow to be tall as the trees?

NOSN You will grow to be as pure and innocent as a dove.

ZIYZI And you won't go home?

NOSN The disaster has reached our home.

ZIYZI Why do you say we have to hide?!

NOSN It is too dangerous to be at home.

ZIYZI Why?

NOSN It is dangerous to have contact with other people.

ZIYZI I'm not going into the forest with you. There are wolves.

NOSN No one will harm you. Do you hear the birds singing? Come and you'll see birds' nests perched on branches swinging back and forth in the wind … You will see baby chicks there; they are not afraid at all.

ZIYZI So we won't go home tonight?

NOSN My children have deserted me.

ZIYZI Will Daddy and Tomer also grow wolves' teeth?

NOSN Don't ask me that! It makes my blood run cold. *(We hear the rumbling of thunder)* This is the first sign … I raised children! I planted trees, I nurtured them with dew from heaven—what is this wind that is causing their roots to wither? … This wind that's snapping off my branches?

ZIYZI Take me home!

NOSN I am here with you.

ZIYZI In the forest we can build a nest in a tree and live there. I will help you climb up into it.

NOSN That's right.

ZIYZI But then we'll go home. I want to see Daddy and Tomer again.

NOSN There is no one at home.

ZIYZI *Zeyde*, you're playing a trick on me! Take me home. If not, I'll leave you here and run back by myself; I'll find my way without you.

NOSN I have raised a snake in my very own bosom, and now it is in our home. If you go back there alone, it will bite you along the way.

Lightening strikes repeatedly.

ZIYZI It's getting even darker. Tomer! Tomer!

NOSN Quiet! No one must know we are here.

ZIYZI is quiet. It becomes darker.

NOSN Alone like a tree that has been cut down, its branches broken …

ZIYZI Come, *Zeyde,* hold my hand.

We hear voices in the distance.

NOSN Human voices. Human animals …

ZIYZI Tomer! Tomer!

The voices get closer.

NOSN I must hide.

Lightening strikes.

ZIYZI Tomer! Tomer!

ZIYZI lets go of NOSN's hand.

NOSN Come with me, my child.

ZIYZI I'm afraid …

NOSN Come, we must leave....

ZIYZI Let me stay, let me stay here!

NOSN I will protect you ... Come with me.

ZIYZI Let me go, let go ...

ZIYZI pulls herself away from him.

NOSN I am not as strong as you are.

NOSN rushes off alone into the forest. ZIYZI remains there for a long time and starts to cry. Thunder rumbles. A bolt of lightening reveals HIYMEN on the hill carrying TOMER in his arms.

ZIYZI Who is that?

HIYMEN It's your sister.

TOMER Sister ... let me down, lay me down on the ground, I don't want you to carry me any more....

ZIYZI Tomer! ... Tomer! ...

TOMER How did you get here, darling?

HIYMEN How did she get here on such an awful night?

TOMER Put me down.

HIYMEN *(To ZIYZI)* Don't be afraid, you'll come with me.

TOMER On the ground ...

ZIYZI cries.

HIYMEN Don't cry. Your life is just beginning.

TOMER Let me stay here on the ground ... Let me die before my father arrives ... I don't want to see him suffer.

HIYMEN puts her down on the ground.

HIYMEN I'll carry you far away from your father's house. Come—life is waiting for you on the other side of the mountain …

TOMER *(To ZIYZI)* Sit down next to me, give me your hands … I will protect you as long as my heart beats … Where is Father?

ZIYZI I don't know.

TOMER Didn't you see him?

ZIYZI No.

TOMER Where is *Zeyde*?

ZIYZI Far away from here—in the forest, he wouldn't let me go home … He wanted to take me with him but I wouldn't go.

TOMER *Zeyde*! Take me to Father … I'm dying.… Go … I want to die alone … I don't want you to hear what I have to say … I don't want you to laugh at me …

HIYMEN I promise not to laugh or cry.

TOMER I spread open my arms hoping they would embrace the whole world.

ZIYZI Who did this to you? Tell me …

HIYMEN I stood in the distance, my heart burned with sorrow. Out of love they bit into your flesh and out of love they trampled you under their feet …

TOMER I ran … I pleaded—"Look, your own sick children lie neglected; one world for everyone … a single sun for everyone" …—No one heard me …

ZIYZI I hear rumbling.

TOMER It's getting closer … and closer.

HIYMEN My child, think it over!

ZIYZI Are you alright, Tomer?

TOMER — My poor sister … I ran, cried—people, people … Who has planted hatred in your heart? Who has placed a spear in your hand? Darkness has come over the world … Stop! Stop! … Mercy … mercy … mercy …

HIYMEN — *(Laughs quietly)* Love, mercy …

TOMER manages to stand up and then falls down again.

TOMER — Go away … go … go! … I will go back … but not you … I will not ask for your mercy … I hate you … I hate you … no … I pity you. Everyone … my father … why is he still at home? It's so late, where is he? Has a spear pierced his heart, too? People! Have respect for my father … his heart goes out to you … respect him! … he has found the true path for you … he has found it … *(Pause)* I have been so foolish … foolish … foolish …

HIYMEN — True … true …

TOMER — No! That is not me speaking! No! Not me … until the last moment … with my last strength I will call out mercy … mercy … love … love …

TOMER dies.

ZIYZI — Tomer … Tomer … Tomer …

HIYMEN — Come with me … Don't be afraid. I will take you with me.

ZIYZI — *Zeyde! Zeyde*! Tomer, wake up! Tomer, wake up!

NODOV — *(From offstage)* My children! My daughter!

ZIYZI — Tomer, Tomer, Daddy's coming!

HIYMEN — Foolish brother! Foolish man!

NODOV — *(From offstage)* My child! I am coming with you … wait, wait!

ZIYZI Here I am, Daddy! Tomer … Tomer!

There is thunder. NODOV enters.

NODOV Are you all here?

HIYMEN Your younger child and your brother.

NODOV Where is my other child?

HIYMEN The beloved people have trampled your child.… Coarse fingers have torn her heart to shreds.

NODOV My daughter.…

HIYMEN I lifted her out of the mud with my own hands …

NODOV I've now come to a fork in the path that I have followed with such certainty. Which way should I go? Mercy has been drowned in a sea of human blood … My child, you have blocked my path like a boulder—I can not get past you … I can go no further. *(Lies down on top of TOMER's body)* My child! You have taken the best of me with you … and it cannot be brought back … The light of my life has been lost in the dark night … like a pure flame you have been extinguished by the angry wind.

ZIYZI Daddy, Daddy! Take me home.

HIYMEN Listen to me, my brother! I didn't say a word while she was still alive, I did that for her.… I will drown out the stale ideas you never outgrew and for which you sacrificed your daughter … I will drown out the cry of your heart that set you on your foolish path … And even as you lie prostrate over your daughter's dead body, taking your final breath—the last spark of warmth that still burns deep inside you will hear me … Listen! Foolish brother! The people of the earth will drown in their own blood … The last survivor will consume his own flesh like a hungry beast—and drink his own blood with devilish thirst.—Don't be the last one!

ZIYZI Daddy, Daddy!

NODOV gets up off of TOMER's body.

NODOV When sorrow becomes more than human strength can bear—the truth must appear … As I lay on my child's cold body a ray of light appeared to me—truth itself … I did not hear what you were saying. The wind carried your words away; the night swallowed them … I'm going, I'm coming! Heaven and earth have melded; stars wallow in the mud, trampled by calloused feet. Youth has lost its heart, age has lost its wisdom … The boundaries established by the God of old have been removed and new ones are not yet in place … People have torn themselves away from the earth but they cannot reach the heavens … *(We hear thunder)* The heavens thunder, the earth quakes; mountains explode … Fire and water pour forth and flow together … Once again, the God of old appears on the earth. He drapes the world in light … His messengers precede him, they ride on the wings of the wind … My God—Here I come! Here I come!

We hear an echo in the distance: "Come."

HIYMEN It is not my God calling.

The wind tears through the forest, the entire forest undulates.

NODOV I hear his voice beckoning, he is calling me … God's voice thunders from one pole of life to the other … In a fever, people are once again obedient … I hear the voice … He calls: "People, cease your perpetual state of war! Mend your thoughts!—Soften your hearts!"—My God, here I come! Here I come!

An echo is heard in the distance: "Come! Come!

HIYMEN It is not my God calling …

NODOV I hear you, my God! … I hear …!! …

We hear an echo of: "Hear!" A storm breaks in the forest.

NODOV Stand in awe, children of the earth. There is a fire, and with sorrow it consumes the heart out of which evil grows. A cloud approaches and carries His lightening—He will pour out his sorrow on the heads of those who have gone astray … *(The storm grows stronger, it whistles; the forest groans. NODOV's voice gets stronger)* Stand in awe! Stand in awe! God is coming. He is spreading His wings over the entire earth! He cloaks both hill and valley in fear … man-children are bowing down! … The ear awaits God's command … my God, I am coming! I am coming!

NODOV exits. ZIYZI remains frozen still. HIYMEN watches NODOV leave.

HIYMEN *(Laughs)* He's gone to find a God—for whom! Fish swallow one another, but not lions, raised in the desert. People must become like lions.

ZIYZI Daddy! Daddy!

HIYMEN takes her by the hand.

HIYMEN Don't cry, don't cry. This is no place for you. I will take you to the highest mountain so that your youth may bloom—there where the eagles are …

HIYMEN carries her off quickly. There is lighting. The sound of the thunder becomes fainter. All we now see is

TOMER's dead body in her white dress. NOSN emerges from the forest.

NOSN Alone ... alone ... like an uprooted tree whose branches have broken off—I will wander aimlessly in the dark night. *(He trips over TOMER)* Who is this? My child ...! Your blood is cold ... *(Sits near her, speaking coldly and with resignation)* Age and despair have made my heart grow cold, and the life in your young heart has been snuffed out ... I will not feel sorry for youth, when old age is filled with fear and darkness. And I will not feel sorry for your lifeless eyes, because my eyes have yet to behold your father's broken heart. I can not feel sorry for either of you, when I have yet to learn whether your sister's bones will come pouring forth from the mountain top ... Your entire life, your heart has never known peace ... I will find a peaceful place for your bones.

NOSN struggles into the forest. There is a bolt of lightening.

CURTAIN

The Amulet (Af Yenem Zayt Taykh)

By Peretz Hirschbein

Translated from Yiddish by Ellen Perecman and Mark Altman

Adapted by Ellen Perecman, Mark Altman and Clay McLeod Chapman

Characters

MENASHE	Ferryman, blind
YAKHNE	His wife
MIYRL	Their granddaughter
A VOICE/STRANGER	
TOWNSPEOPLE	

Act One

A wooden house on a riverbank. There is a stove, a table, a few unpainted chairs, and a bed. It is the middle of the night. We hear the rushing of water, the crashing of floating ice. Wind rattles at the windows. A candle burns on the stove.

There is a prolonged silence.

MENASHE — It'll be a long time before we ever see summer! The wind just keeps on whistling. Endlessly, endlessly … Miyrl, are you asleep?

MIYRL — *(From offstage)* I thought you were sleeping, *Zeyde*. What's keeping you awake?

MENASHE — I'm listening to what I can't see. The ice is breaking up, sweeping the floes downriver, one after another … At this time of year I used to love to take the little boat across the river. The ice floe rushed as if it were pursuing someone, but I outran her. I was able to predict her path, though she could never predict mine. The whole trick is in outwitting her—in the blink of an eye, to decide whether to steer right or left. Now there's no more ferry … That smell. Is something burning?

MIYRL — There's a candle on the table.

MENASHE Everything looks even darker than usual to me today. Life is coated with a black tar. Even my white beard looks as black as in my youth. Ah, youth …

MIYRL Do you hear the river churning? It's terrifying! What would happen if the ferry were on the river right now, *Zeyde*?

MENASHE Why would it be there?

MIYRL It could have been taken ashore for the winter …

MENASHE The ice floes would smash it to bits. An ice floe may not be very strong on its own, but with a whole river behind it … water is not to be underestimated. It is strong. You wouldn't remember this … but under that little hill there, in the clay area, there were once three houses. One belonged to the nobleman. And when the river went wild, it demolished them all. In fact, it was that year the *tzadik*—the holy man—passed through. His eyes drank it all in—his mind made sense of everything. Nothing escaped him …

MIYRL I'm coming out.

MENASHE I'd rather you sleep, *mayn kiynd.*

MIYRL I can't sleep. Not with the windows right on the river. There is such rumbling and roaring.—Can't you hear it? Is it tearing the roof off?

MENASHE He noticed everything. "There's no happiness in those three houses,"—the Holy Man said to his aide as they passed by. "In one"—he said "the foundation was built lower than the others and the roof higher." That was the nobleman's house.

MIYRL *Zeyde,* did the water ever carry a ferry away?

MENASHE We wouldn't let such things happen. There'd be no end to it if we did. When the river starts rising, how do you stop it? How could you? It did happen once …, but that was in the middle of the summer. Long ago.

MIYRL enters wrapped in a shawl.

MIYRL — I want to sit next to you, *Zeyde*. I won't be able to sleep anyway. Tell me what happened when the river carried the ferry away.

MENASHE — It was the middle of summer. It poured all summer long. There was a famine that year. Everything got moldy and spoiled. And when the rain had flooded the river, it broke free and grabbed the ferry. Just picked it up and whisked it away … Yes, I remember it as if it happened yesterday.

MIYRL — It must have been beautiful. Watching the water carry it away …

MENASHE — Such things are not at all beautiful. May God only protect us from water. Where are you? Where have you gone? Sit closer to me!

MIYRL — Are you cold, *Zeyde*?

MENASHE — No, *mayn kiynd*. When you were born, my sight was already failing; I saw you only in shadows. With God's grace, you've grown from a tiny mite to a young woman—but I can't see you. You take after your mother, you know that? I still remember her face. She was as radiant as the sun. So full of goodness … No one compared with her … So it is, one waits a whole lifetime for some good fortune. And when it finally comes, she's gone. Your mother did everything in her power to earn God's kindness. She gave to charity. She was kind. She consulted miracle workers for amulets and blessings.

MENASHE pats MIYRL'S chest in search of something.

MIYRL — What are you looking for, *Zeyde*?

MENASHE — I want to see whether you're wearing her amulet.

MIYRL pulls out an amulet tied to a ribbon.

MIYRL — Here it is, tied to a ribbon ... Will you tell me what's inside? Please?

MENASHE — Your happiness lies inside. You must guard it with your life. It will protect you from harm. God decided your mother did not deserve to see what she had been waiting for her entire life. Death seized her the moment you entered the world. She never even saw you, death had already closed her eyes ... but in her heart, she understood how lucky she was. There was a smile on her lips as they lowered her into the grave.

MIYRL — My mother never even saw me?

MENASHE — No, *mayn kiynd*, her eyes were already closed.

MIYRL — She died because of me?

MENASHE — For you; you were her treasure and she never even saw you.

MIYRL — She died for me?

MENASHE — It was just before Pesach. The river was as rough as it is today. The water was dark and covered with foam. You could barely see the top of the tree, opposite the bridge. Minute by minute, the water rose, and minute by minute our joy multiplied. Your mother wanted to carry a baby in her arms. Your father was looking for solace after a long day of work—and I just wanted to *shep nakhes* from all of you.... The rushing of the water became stronger and stronger, and as the tree became entirely hidden from view, the whole area became a turbulent sea. Our happiness grew—your mother went into labor with you ... that would be the end of our happiness. Just as now, the wind howled then too. The ice continued to shatter. And when the water level finally fell—tragedy had made its way through the window and through the door ... It took five days—five terrifying days. Joy mixed with horror. Our hearts pounded with fear and excitement. And when the water finally retreated, your mother had been consumed by the terrible wrath.

MIYRL — *Zeyde,* do you hear the river rushing again? Just like you said. Look at it! The water is so high! Earlier today, the base of the tree near the bridge was covered.

MENASHE — The water carried everything off. It swept it all away! It took your *tate* and your *mame* away from you; it took away my sight … Can you really see the water touching the tree?

MIYRL — Absolutely. With my own eyes.

MENASHE — Has it overflowed its banks?

MIYRL — Can't you hear it rumbling?

MENASHE hugs her.

MENASHE — My arms can feel how much you've grown.

MIYRL — I want to tell you something, *Zeyde*!

MENASHE — What, *mayn kiynd*?

MIYRL — Last night I dreamt that I was sleeping on the ferry boat. It was summer. A young woman tried to take my amulet from me. She wore a sunhat … I remember her sunhat. She approached me so quietly. Could it have been my *mame*?

MENASHE — She tried to take your amulet from you?

MIYRL — Yes.

MENASHE — Why didn't you tell me right away?

MIYRL — Sometimes I feel like opening it to see what's inside.

MENASHE — What are you saying?!

MIYRL — Sometimes I wonder what could be inside.…

MENASHE It was your *mame* who came to you in the dream. Word had spread that you were thinking about committing a grave sin. Your *mame* learned about it in Heaven. A terrible idea planted itself in your heart ... One with the power to upset the heavens, God forbid!

MIYRL *Zeyde*, did *Mame* wear a sunhat?

MENASHE No one knows who the *tzadik* was. Whenever I think of him, the sun brings light to my eyes and I see as clear as day—. Passing through here, he blessed us with one hand and cursed us with the other. With one he punished and with the other he brought comfort. In His beloved name, we must accept everything joyfully. You do not wear the amulet over your heart but rather in your heart. In it lies your happiness. Heaven and earth may—God forbid—tremble if you touch what is inside.

MENASHE stands up and goes to the window.

MIYRL Where are you going, *Zeyde*?

MENASHE The river is roaring louder than usual ...

MIYRL Do you see something, *Zeyde*?

MENASHE The light in my eyes has gone out. Only when His holy face appears to me, is there light ...

MIYRL I am afraid, *Zeyde*!

MENASHE Don't be afraid, *mayn kiynd*. His divine name will protect you. Without misfortune there can be no good fortune ... Wrath has now run its course. Without eyes, I am as if dead. What more can He do to me? He has taken my daughter from me. The river has taken your father. I've reached the end. But God's kindness awaits you ... And listen! The river is roaring louder than usual ...

MIYRL *Zeyde*, maybe it's because I ...

MENASHE — Your heart is still pure. Your thoughts are innocent. Children are only punished for their parents' sins. Your *mame* left this world pure as an angel; your *tate* died a martyr's death. God has no reason to punish you. Are you dressed warmly enough? Do you have your shoes on?

MIYRL — Why, *Zeyde*?

MENASHE — I want you to take me outside. It is time for me to see how high the river has risen!

MIYRL — It's as high as the branches.

MIYRL exits. The wind is whipping fiercely.

MENASHE — The wind is gusting so fiercely … Where are you, *mayn kiynd*?

MIYRL reenters.

MIYRL — Come *Zeyde*, hold on to me.

MENASHE — It must be very late. Even the roosters have gone to bed. The cry of the rooster makes a dark night feel safe.

MIYRL — *Zeyde*! All this talk frightens me …

MENASHE — Who are you afraid of, *mayn kiynd*?

MIYRL — I don't know. The wind … The river …

MENASHE — Are you taking me outside?

MIYRL — You've never spoken like this before, *Zeyde*.

MENASHE — Every time the ice breaks and frees the floes, when the water spills over the banks, I await destiny, yours and mine. Take me outside. *(They start to go outside)* Are you dressed warmly enough?

They go outside. The whipping of the wind and the rumbling of the water intensifies. The wind blows out the light. We hear MENASHE's voice through the door.

MENASHE — This is beyond imagination.

MENASHE goes back inside. MIYRL follows him.

MIYRL — *Zeyde*? The water is about to come into the house …

MENASHE — Does the river really intend to carry away my four walls? Miyrl! Take me back outside, I have to feel it with my own hands. I don't believe it. Take me outside!

MIYRL — I can't take you any further. My feet are soaking wet …

MENASHE — For one moment, dear God, give me back my sight … Just for one moment!

MIYRL — Let's get away from here.

MENASHE — Log by log, I built these walls. Straw by straw, I thatched the roof. Here I was born into happiness, but grew old into sadness … For just one moment, Ruler of the Universe, I beg you—please return my sight to me.

MIYRL — It's dark—I may not be able to find my way out.

MENASHE — Can the water have reached these walls?! I must see it for myself … Take me outside again, Miyrl.

There is a loud bang on the wall.

MIYRL — *Zeyde*, did you hear that? Something crashed against the wall. Somebody just looked in the window …

MENASHE — What do you think you saw in the window? Where are you?

MIYRL — I think—someone's speaking. I hear … in the wind … Earlier you talked about these things and now I must be imagining them.

MENASHE: I cannot leave this house. I must not. Where are you?

MIYRL: I've closed my eyes so I don't see the window. Someone is out there in the darkness.

There is a second bang on the wall.

MENASHE: Who's banging? Can it be that the river has risen so high that the ice floes are crashing into my house?—Can the water have risen so quickly? Take me outside! …

MIYRL: I won't go, *Zeyde.* I can't move. My feet are frozen to the spot …

MENASHE: He said: After the greatest tragedy, happiness will appear … Who can fathom the depths of tragedy?! Where does it end? When my daughter died, I thought I had drunk the cup dry. But then the light in my eyes went out. And after that the river swallowed your father.

MIYRL: *Zeyde*, hush! I think I see my *mame* …

MENASHE: *Mayn kiynd*! Open your eyes. God took the light from my eyes. He gave you that light. Open your eyes and take your *zeyde* outside.

MIYRL moves toward the wall.

MIYRL: Stay where you are, *Zeyde*!

MENASHE: Who is frightening you, *mayn kiynd*?

MIYRL: Stay away from me!

MENASHE: I don't recognize your voice! Your voice has changed. Where are you? Take my hand; I am still your *zeyde*, the one who took the brunt of God's punishment. Your soul is pure. It has been purified many times over. We all sacrificed for you. Come here.

MIYRL stands at the wall and stares at him silently.

MENASHE Where are you? … Why don't you answer me … Where are you?! Why has your sweet voice fallen silent? …

MIYRL *Zeyde*! Close your eyes. Your dark stare scares me … Please close them …

MENASHE I see a shining sun in the corner there. There is a warm glow coming from the amulet around your neck. I can see every inch of the house. *(He goes to where MIYRL is standing)* Now I see you, *mayn kiynd*. I see you standing there trembling.

MIYRL sinks back against the wall.

MENASHE What does this mean? Do you want to abandon your old *zeyde*? Come, I want to hold on to you. Your soul is pure—protect me too. Please—I beg you! I see Eden's light on your breast. The rays of His divine name.

MIYRL *(Looking in fear at her amulet) Zeyde*, I'm going to touch it!

MENASHE Who is speaking these words? …

MIYRL I can't stand it anymore. I'm taking it off.

MENASHE *Mayn kiynd*! The earth is crumbling beneath my feet! The heavens are splitting! …

MIYRL exits.

MENASHE The river is seething with anger. Covered with foam … it is rising. Where are you? I pray your *mame* will save you.—Her soul must be pure by now. Your father, his soul is certainly pure! He died a martyr's death.

MIYRL reenters and climbs onto the stove.

MENASHE Where are you, *mayn kiynd*? Has your voice been silenced?

MIYRL tries to rip the amulet from her breast.

MENASHE The light has suddenly gone out! ... Where are you?! Why don't you say something?! Please—please tell me you haven't done an unspeakable thing—please come back! You've removed the radiance from your heart. *(There is a loud bang on the wall)* The earth is trembling with sorrow. Angry spirits have begun to circle my home ... It's dark everywhere. Have you left the house? ... *(There is again a bang on the wall)* Holy angels! Save me, *mayn kiynd*! The water is at my feet! Is the river thrusting its waves into my house? What have you done?!

MIYRL *Zeyde*! The house is flooding!

MENASHE You have upset the heavens. The cup of wrath is spilling over.

MENASHE opens the door, the water pours into the house, the wind howls, blowing out the candle.

MIYRL *Zeyde*! You've made the light go out! ... We're drowning!

MENASHE *(Moving toward MIYRL)* Help me! Your light is shining again ... Come forth holy angels!

MIYRL *Zeyde*, be quiet ... I see something in the window ... I see the water rising; be quiet ... We're drowning!

MENASHE It's getting brighter. I see the heavens opening. I see His countenance. He's coming to rescue me. I am sure ... Where are you, *mayn kiynd*?

The wind howls, the ice floes bang against the wall.

MIYRL *Zeyde*, I'm getting out.

MIYRL jumps off of the stove. We hear a splash.

MENASHE I'll follow you. I'll follow....

There is silence. Soft rays begin to stream through the window in the house. The water in the house looks as though it is illuminated by the moon.

MIYRL Something is calling to us. It is waving us on ... Beckoning ...

MENASHE I feel warm rays falling on me.

MIYRL They are telling us to hurry.

MENASHE I see day breaking.

MIYRL The water is up to my knees. I'm going out through the window, straight to the lights.

MENASHE It's Him with His messengers coming to greet you. You must go directly to the lights ...

MIYRL opens the window and climbs out. MENASHE makes his way slowly to the window.

MENASHE How miraculous! I feel warm even among the ice floes. Light—in the dark night. *Mayn kiynd* don't leave me! ...

MENASHE climbs out the window. Silence. The light disappears. Darkness. The wind rips through the windows and doors. The ice floes slam from all sides. The walls creak. The roof caves in. We hear a roar of the water and the house collapses with a terrifying noise.

Act Two

Night. The wind blows large clouds. The moonlight shines through the clouds and we see a hill covered in trees. We hear the splashing of the water. From time to time, the wind carries tragic calls for help from the distance. From offstage, we hear MENASHE's voice getting closer and closer.

MENASHE — Alone … all alone, just me and my useless eyes. Dry! I've made it to a hill … Dear God! You have not abandoned me.… Dry ground. I'll climb higher, to the top; I will be safe there.

MENASHE now appears in the pale light of the moon. MIYRL follows him quietly.

MENASHE — The water has soaked through my clothes. Me—an old ferry boat captain … I've always known how to avoid danger; where can I warm my freezing body?

MIYRL goes to a corner and sits quietly shivering from the cold.

MENASHE — I hear voices in the distance. Could it be her voice? She's upset the heavens. Now that I can feel my body again, it's as if she has been severed from me. I don't feel her body against mine any longer.

We hear a splash in the water.

MENASHE Miyrl! … Miyrl! … I have frightened her away with my words. She frightened me with her thoughts. I am safe from the flood. But something is missing, everything is missing … I'd be so much warmer if she were here with me now … Her eyes would have enough light for the two of us. Her youth would drive away my old age. Miyrl!….

MIYRL goes closer to him and stands in front of him.

MENASHE What has happened to the light I followed with such confidence? Come back! … I feel warmer just thinking of her. But oh—how I'd feel even warmer if she were sitting right here at my side.

MIYRL *Zeyde*, why are you crying?

MENASHE Who is that? … Who is there? Answer! *(The moonlight falls on MENASHE)* I feel light pouring over these old bones. If I open my eyes wider, perhaps I'll see something. Who is talking? Where am I? Safer but still in darkness. The wind carried her voice to me, telling me to rescue her? … *(MENASHE tries to walk and immediately falls)* My legs are frozen, frozen to the knees. My heart beat is fading.

MIYRL stands even closer to him.

MIYRL Don't cry, *Zeyde*.

MENASHE Miyrl! Is that your voice? Are you close by?

MENASHE crawls on all fours.

MIYRL I am not far away, *Zeyde*.

MENASHE *Mayn kiynd*! I hear your voice clearly. Are you cold?—Then come to me. I will warm you with my old heart. Come, I want to put my arms around you.

MIYRL I'm cold. *Zeyde …*

MENASHE stands up, and then falls down again.

MENASHE You must come to me. I will give you my last flicker of warmth.

MIYRL I will only come if you promise you won't frighten me.

MENASHE I can hear you shivering—come closer.…

MIYRL throws herself into his arms.

MIYRL Here I am, *Zeyde*, warm me!

MENASHE I will warm you with my heart. Give me your feet. I will warm them with my breath …

MIYRL Where are we, *Zeyde*?

MENASHE I think we're far away from the flood. But we're not protected from the wind. I followed the light, and you used my sightless eyes as a compass … Are you warmer now, *mayn kiynd*?

MIYRL It's cold. Even under your cloak, it's bitter. The wind is piercing right through.

MENASHE Move closer to me then.

MIYRL I heard our house collapse. Where will we go now?

MENASHE We will surrender our hearts and bodies to God.

MIYRL You marched off as if you knew where you were going.

MENASHE My body is getting colder, but my heart only grows warmer.

MIYRL When the sun rises again, we'll look for our house.

MENASHE *Mayn kiynd*!

MIYRL Don't frighten me! I must get warm.

MENASHE I don't feel the beating of your heart …

MIYRL *Zeyde*, I am going back to the flood—if you don't stop talking like that!

MENASHE I feel as though a piece of ice is pressing against my heart …

MIYRL Talk to me as you did at home. That will warm me again …

MENASHE It's freezing … cold … cold …

MIYRL Hush, *Zeyde*. I want to pretend that we're sleeping and I'm cuddling next to you.

MENASHE Take my hands and place them on your heart. I can't move them. I want to see … I want …

MIYRL Be quiet … be quiet …

MENASHE I want to find the true light over your heart.

MIYRL I lost the amulet in the flood.

MENASHE You … lost it?!

MIYRL Someone tore it off my neck …

MENASHE Lost … We've drunk the cup of wrath empty, but happiness was not there waiting for us. It's becoming difficult to move my mouth.

MIYRL Here, I will cover you.

MIYRL throws her wrap over him.

MENASHE The *tzadiyk*! His saintly face appears before me … Who are you going to save—me or my child? … Have pity …

MIYRL takes off another item of clothing and covers him with it.

MENASHE — The warm wings of heavenly angels embrace me ... Burning eyes peer into my heart ... Warmer ... Warmer ...

VOICE — *(From off-stage as if carried from afar by the wind)* S-a-v-e m-e! I'm drowning.

MIYRL — Over here! It's dry here!

MENASHE — From Heaven I hear the voices of angels ... from Paradise the holy song pours forth ...

VOICE — *(The Voice is closer)* S-a-v-e m-e, I am freezing!

MIYRL — Over here! It's dry.

MENASHE — I see you my daughter! ... You are amongst the righteous ... you have come to me from heaven. Your face is radiant ... Your eyes sparkle like stars ... Warmer ... Warmer ...

VOICE — *(The Voice is very close)* W-h-e-r-e s-h-o-u-l-d I g-o?

MIYRL — Straight ahead! Straight ahead!

MENASHE — They're singing God's praises in heaven ... It's dawn ... The heavens have awoken. The *tzadiyk* joins the angels in singing God's praises ...

We hear water splashing.

VOICE — Are there people there?

MIYRL looks out into the distance.

MENASHE — *(Chanting)* The light of day is upon us ... God's kindness is near. I sing his praises. I give reverence to his creations ...

VOICE — Who is there? Identify yourselves!

MIYRL Over here!

We see a figure shivering in the cold.

MENASHE *(Chanting)* His ineffable name … his kindness and mercy …

STRANGER Who is there?

MIYRL We are.

STRANGER People? There are people here?

MIYRL The flood drove us here, the water came up to our necks.

STRANGER Who is that over there?

MIYRL My *zeyde*. He's freezing to death.

STRANGER Freezing?

MIYRL He can't get warm.

STRANGER *(Bends over MENASHE)* Frozen, he's dead …

MIYRL Oh, *Zeyde*!

STRANGER There is no sign of life. We will be gone by daylight too if we don't find warmth soon.

MIYRL Oh, *Zeyde, Zeyde*, wake up! *Zeyde*, I know where the amulet is!

STRANGER Your attempts to wake him are useless. You will never revive him. It would be best if we warmed each other until morning …

MIYRL *Zeyde!… Zeyde!… Zeyde*! … You've left me alone in the dark … *Zeyde*!

STRANGER There is no life left in your grandfather. Come away from him. He reeks of cold and terror.

MIYRL I will lie down next to him and die …

STRANGER Your grandfather died because the blood in his veins froze long ago … I will not let you die, now that I have survived.

MIYRL *Zeyde*! Take me with you! …

STRANGER The river carried me all night. I clung to the prow of a shattered ferry. I wouldn't let go no matter how cold my limbs grew. It flung me onto this hill … I don't even know how far it carried me.—But I sensed that it brought me to the other side of the river … Come closer. Come to me. Let's warm each other …

MIYRL I don't know you … I musn't … I want to sit next to my *Zeyde* and freeze to death.

STRANGER Whether you like it or not, I'll warm you and you me. What's that covering the old man? Dry clothes … He doesn't need them anymore. Let's take them from him.

MIYRL Don't you touch him!

STRANGER You can't warm someone who's frozen. The dead don't need warmth—like we do. Come. Come here. You will see your desire to live grow as we wait for morning … There's no use trying to revive a frozen corpse … Come to me, you're shivering. Look at how our teeth are chattering … Come, let's press our bodies together for warmth. When morning comes, we'll search for shelter … Come here!

MIYRL I'm afraid …

STRANGER Of what?

MIYRL Of you.

STRANGER Me? Don't be afraid of me. I'm just a human being … The floodwater brought me here. To you. It's dark. I can't tell you from where I've come from, because I have no idea where I am.

MIYRL Cold … It's so cold … I can feel myself freezing to death.

STRANGER You seek death for no good reason. Life is calling us. It is almost morning. Come to me. Don't be afraid of me. You don't have enough warmth left in you to withstand the cold and neither do I. We can give each other the gift of life … But first you have to put your arms around me.

MIYRL *Zeyde* is dead.

STRANGER And we must live!

STRANGER embraces her tightly.

MIYRL Leave me alone … leave me …

STRANGER I will force you to live! I will force you to give me life! Pull me close to you …

MIYRL My *zeyde*'s blind eyes are staring at me … The amulet … Let me go! … The *tzadiyk* …

STRANGER Your *zeyde* is dead … we must live … tighter, that's it … tighter …

MIYRL A stream of warm blood just ran through my veins!

STRANGER Life is returning to you. I am from the other side of the river. From there I have brought you life.

MIYRL I can feel my limbs again!

STRANGER Let's press our hearts together. Then we'll be warm.

MIYRL Our teeth are no longer chattering!

STRANGER Your voice is no longer quivering.

MIYRL Perhaps we can try to warm *Zeyde*?

STRANGER Ice cannot be warmed.

MIYRL I'm beginning to have hope.

STRANGER Your youth has melted the blood in my veins.

MIYRL I lost the amulet. My *zeyde* told me I should always keep it over my heart. My *zeyde* …

STRANGER Death was stronger than he was. We shall live … Wait!

MIYRL What do you hear?

STRANGER I hear your heart beating with joy.

MIYRL I'm starting to feel so warm.

STRANGER My clothes were frozen stiff—like armor. Yours too. But under that armor, there was a flicker of life …

MIYRL When I used to cuddle up to *Zeyde,* I never felt this warm. Right before you came, I held my body close to his, but it only made me colder.

STRANGER Do you see the gray strip over there to the left?

MIYRL On the ground?

STRANGER No, in the sky.

MIYRL What is happening?

STRANGER Day is breaking. Soon there will be light and we can look for shelter.

MIYRL I have nowhere to go. The flood carried our house away. I watched it drift off without us … My *zeyde* froze to death.

STRANGER Go towards life. Life will lead you to a new home. You must have had a little wooden house, if the flood was able to carry it away—Life will lead you to palaces … Beautiful palaces and golden castles decorated with pearls and rubies. Floods will never be able to reach them! And neither will fire … You see, the cold may have turned your *zeyde* to ice, but it has no power over us.

MIYRL My *zeyde* always spoke to me differently. Every evening he would speak to me—but differently than you. I used to put my head in his lap, and he would tell me stories … I understood him better than I understand you. But his words never made me feel so warm. It was never cold in our house. The wind never blew inside …

STRANGER Do you feel life beating like a drum in your veins?

MIYRL Yes …

STRANGER Do you feel your blood surging like the river that swept away the houses and brought me to you?

MIYRL Yes …

STRANGER You don't always have to understand—it's better to feel.

MIYRL I had been afraid of my *zeyde*. He used to stare at me through his blind eyes. Something peered out of them and scared me.

STRANGER Oh, your *zeyde* was blind!—Death itself peered out of his eyes and frightened you.

MIYRL He was blind but he walked here on his own. I followed him. He reached this hill by himself.

STRANGER Death was leading him; it lit his way with a black fire.

MIYRL I saw the fire too. I was also drawn to it. I thought that it was the *tzadiyk*. The angels *Zeyde* always talked about. Even the tips of my fingers are warm.… Look, daylight!

STRANGER Keep your eyes closed a little longer and feel … Do you see something?

MIYRL I see beautiful palaces on a tall hill …

STRANGER They will all be yours.

MIYRL Who do they belong to now?

STRANGER To no one. Life builds them and whoever wants them can have them.

MIYRL When I close my eyes I feel as though I am sitting in heaven, with angels flying around me. It is as bright as *Zeyde* said it was.

STRANGER Your *zeyde* could only dream about a world after death. It can be yours in life … Look, it's already quite light. I can see the whole area. Most of it is still covered with water. But there. See it? There's a narrow strip of dry ground to the left. It reaches to the hill we are on. We can take that path out of here.

MIYRL I will keep my eyes closed and you keep talking … talking …

STRANGER And you?

MIYRL I will feel.

STRANGER Do you feel anything?

MIYRL I feel everything … I feel, I see, I feel, I see …

STRANGER That's good. But the path down from here is a long one … It is day. We will soon leave. Pressed body against body we will walk—and along the way, I will tell you beautiful stories.

MIYRL And what about my *zeyde*?

STRANGER Those who tend to the dead will come and bury him.

MIYRL I should leave him?

STRANGER We will ask those who tend to the dead to come and bury him

MIYRL But he's my *zeyde*!

STRANGER stands up and takes hold of her tightly.

MIYRL Where are you taking me?!

STRANGER Towards life, come!

MIYRL Let me go. Something is pulling me to my *zeyde*, I cannot leave him …

STRANGER leads MIYRL away.

STRANGER Come, I will tell you beautiful stories along the way.

MIYRL *Zeyde! Zeyde*! I cannot leave you! …

STRANGER Life is calling—life … I can release you, but I have your soul—And your body will come looking for it …

STRANGER exits down the hill. MIYRL follows him as if in a trance.

MIYRL *Zeyde!* … *Zeyde*! … Save me! … *(She disappears down the hill. Her voice is heard calling: Zeyde! … Zeyde!)*

Act Three

On the river bank. Summer evening. The bank is covered with white sand and long, sparse grass. Here and there a little yellow flower. In the distance, on the other side, one sees the other bank overgrown with saplings. We hear the chirping of birds coming from there. The sun sets and the entire sky is red. Rain clouds are gathering on the other side of the sky. YAKHNE enters from a distance dragging a wooden beam.

YAKHNE — What are you doing there?! Who are you waiting for?!

MIYRL — The river, the dark river frightens me whenever I think about crossing to the other side. And her … What does she want from me?

YAKHNE — It's getting dark. Why are you still here?

MIYRL — Why is she afraid of the night!?

YAKHNE drops the beam.

YAKHNE — What are you doing here, come home. It's getting dark. We have to get up early tomorrow. Even before the rooster crows, we've got to pack up and go see the *tzadiyk*.

MIYRL — Where does the *tzadiyk* come from?

YAKHNE — *(Points away from the river)* From over there.

MIYRL Don't you see, that's where the sun sets everyday and I can't cross the river.

YAKHNE She's lost her mind!

MIYRL Where did that roof beam come from?

YAKHNE What do you think? ... I found it in the field. I recognized it—it's from our house.

MIYRL From our house? Then throw it in the river. Let the water carry it away. Here. I'll do it myself ...

YAKHNE Don't you dare!

MIYRL ... Where are the palaces he told me about? Life offers golden palaces studded with diamonds and rubies ... Without him I will never find them ... Without him I cannot even cross the river. He came from the other side of the river during the night, he appeared in the darkness and warmed my frozen body. *(To YAKHNE)* Go home! I don't want you near me tonight.... Just go—if you won't, then help me build a ferry so I can get to the other side.

YAKHNE I hope your mother begs God to have mercy on you.

MIYRL No. My *mame* was *Zeyde*'s daughter, I'm afraid of her.

YAKHNE May your father pray for you.

MIYRL Leave me be!

YAKHNE If only your fearless *zeyde* could move the heavens with his prayers.

MIYRL If you won't stop talking, I'm going to jump into the river. Where the water is black and murky ... How sweet is the music of those trees—everything is on the other side. The trees sprung up after he disappeared ... Perhaps he planted them? Perhaps he's waiting there for me ...

YAKHNE Let's go. Come, come on—it's about to rain.

MIYRL — I always imagine him coming at night and building a bridge for me to cross, to be able to reach the palaces.

MIYRL pulls up a few yellow flowers and throws them into the river.

MIYRL — Carry them away, water. Straight to him … Tell him I am cold again. Tell him I am freezing again. Like I was that night when the flood brought us to the hill … Tell him that I have kept his warmth in my heart, but I can no longer, I can no longer keep it burning … With its last flicker I will die. I'm turning into a piece of ice just like *Zeyde.* (Beat) What are you waiting for? Did *Zeyde* leave you here on earth to frighten me? Your eyes are as dark as *Zeyde*'s were that night.

YAKHNE — I've got to find people who can take you to the *tzadiyk.*

MIYRL walks along the river bank and sings.

MIYRL — In a ruby palace stands a tall, beautiful throne. He sits there like an angel. Like an angel …

YAKHNE — Look at all the thick clouds filling the sky. Any minute now it's going to rain buckets and you will be out here unprotected.

MIYRL — Any minute now! The clouds are getting thicker, darker. Blacker! It will pour—There will be a flood … It will wash away the bridges as it did the last time when I was just a child … And then the water will bring him back to me. All the palaces—he will bring his whole life with him.

YAKHNE — I hear thunder, let's go quickly. I will not stay here any longer.

MIYRL — I can already hear the thunder. Soon the skies will open. Bright flashes of light will dance.

YAKHNE Evil spirits, angels of destruction! They have surrounded her and won't leave her alone. If only someone would come along, and help me get her home.

MIYRL Oh, if only I could see through the forest on the other side of the river! … He is there somewhere—Come! Come! I feel that you are not far from me—Come! Soon the water will overflow its banks—I feel it. The thunder is announcing its arrival. *(To YAKHNE)* What are you waiting for? Any minute now it will "rain buckets", flooding everywhere. Go! Go then! Go take cover in the house. You want to go to the other side too? There's nothing there for you. You stay here. Go home—go! Why are you standing guard over me? When the river rises I will go to the other side. My arms are pulling me, my legs, my heart is drawn to …! I cannot resist any longer. Darker, darker …

YAKHNE takes an amulet from her neck, quietly approaches MIYRL and puts it around her neck.

YAKHNE Help me, God! Rescue her from these angels of destruction …

MIYRL throws the amulet into the water.

YAKHNE Oh my God! *(She climbs into the river)* What have you done?! … Your mother's daughter …

MIYRL I will let the water carry everything away until I reach the other side.

YAKHNE I've got to find someone to help me … the river is a net just waiting to trap her.

YAKHNE exits.

MIYRL I will cast off everything. *(She pulls the beam to the riverbank and throws it in the water)* Go join the rest of my house. She went to get someone. I will hide … I will submit to the dark night. *(There is a bolt of lightening)* Lightening! No one is here with me … Everything disappears, everything vanishes; everything came to me in the darkness and in the darkness everything is taken away … He took my heart and he left me his … His … My heart has never ached so. My heart has never longed so. He stole my heart and he abandoned me … Perhaps I lost my heart along with the amulet? When I sat with *Zeyde*, I was silent. I was foolish and my heart was calm. (A*nother bolt of lightening)* The sky is angry with me. I wish it would just rain. There is thunder and still no rain … it's getting darker and darker … I see my *zeyde*'s eyes floating before me … They are staring at me from all sides. What do they want of me? Oh, his eyes are signaling … Bright … Shining like two stars. Bright! My *zeyde*'s eyes! What are they asking of me?! The thunder is getting louder. I'm getting cold. The frost is overwhelming me …

YAKHNE *(Offstage)* Grab her. Let's get her out of here.

MIYRL I will not let them! I will not go back! …

YAKHNE enters followed by two TOWNSPEOPLE.

TOWNSPERSON 1 We'll get her to the *tzadiyk* whether she likes it or not. Grab hold of her!

YAKHNE Save my child! Save her!

MIYRL Leave me alone! I have no soul … Let me go back towards life …

TOWNSPERSON 1 Come with me.

MIYRL I will die if you take me from here.

YAKHNE Quickly!

TOWNSPERSON 1 tries to carry MIYRL away.

MIYRL You're killing me! Leave me alone!

YAKHNE Save her, save her!

We hear thunder.

MIYRL You are cutting me off from life … I have wandered so far from my home … *(She sees something in the distance)* You are here! Come quickly. He is calling me! … Come quickly, save me from them. Embrace me as you did that night … I am freezing to death again. Quickly … Please! They are tearing me away from you! … He is coming and with him all the golden palaces; radiant palaces! Here! Here!—

YAKHNE For God's sake, take her away …

TOWNSPERSON 1 What's the matter with the girl?

TOWNSPERSON 2 God is with us! Just grab her.

TOWNSPEOPLE grab MIYRL.

MIYRL Save me! Save me … rescue me …

The TOWNSPEOPLE lead her away. We hear thunder and lightening. MIYRL breaks their hold and runs to the river.

MIYRL You've come! Hold me tighter, tighter … I am leaping into your arms—my joy! My life … Catch me!

MIYRL throws herself in the river. Lightening illuminates the entire area. In the distance we see YAKHNE and the other people running toward the river.

CURTAIN

WITH THE CURRENT (MITN SHTROM)

BY SHOLEM ASCH

Translation from Yiddish by Ellen Perecman, Mark Altman, Yermiyahu Ahron Taub

Adaptation by Ellen Perecman, Mark Altman and Clay McLeod Chapman

Characters

ZOREKH	A rabbi
HINDL	His wife
ROKHL	Their daughter
DOVIYD	Rokhl's husband
YEKHEZKL	Son of Rokhl and Doviyd
VOICE 1	A female voice
VOICE 2	A male voice

Act One

ROKHL, a beautiful young woman in her early 20's, is sitting in the home she shares with her husband and parents. There is a bookcase filled with books on one wall. Her young son, YEKHEZKL, has fallen asleep in her arms. Her mother, HINDL is by her side.

ROKHL *(Singing quietly) "Unter Yekhezhl's viygele, shteyt a klor vays tziygele. Dos tziygele iz geforen handeln. Dos vet zayn dayn baruf…"* He's fallen asleep.

HINDL removes the child's shoes and holy garment[tziytzes]

HINDL Thank goodness. *(To the child)* Such a dangerous world we live in. God protect you. I know you'll grow up to make your parents proud.

ROKHL His mother, at least.

HINDL Wipe those thoughts from your mind, dear. There's nothing to worry about. With God's help—there will never be anything to worry about.

ROKHL Easy for you to say. You don't hear him tossing and turning all night.

HINDL Point taken. Your father says he hasn't been himself lately.

ROKHL Mother—last night he was crying so hard I couldn't sleep. When I went over to his bed, he had his face buried in the pillow. He asked me: "Is that you, Rokhele?" I've never been so frightened in all my life! *(Pause)*

HINDL A wife should always know what's on her husband's mind. She must know, because....

ROKHL How do I get it out of him, Mother? Whenever I ask, he says it's nothing. Always—"It's nothing, Rokhele."

HINDL This isn't about getting it out of him. It's about you figuring it out for yourself ... After your father and I got married, he wanted us to move out of my father's house. Time for him to find his own pulpit. He always moped around. Never said a word. But I knew what was going on. He didn't have to say a thing. I knew. As a wife, you have to know these things.

ROKHL I follow him around. I look into his eyes. I just want him to blurt it out ... Sometimes I feel like he's trying to tell me something. It's there in his eyes—but I just can't figure out what it is. I'm not like you, Mother ...

HINDL Your husband—he's no ordinary man. You know that, right? A very special person. The only hope for the Jewish people ... Maybe this is how such people behave. His way of repenting. Maybe his mind is on things we can't understand. Like it or not—you're his wife. That comes with great responsibility. Prove yourself. Love him. Does he love you? You can tell me. I'm your mother. It's not a sin. It's your responsibility. Only you can make your husband love you.

ROKHL Mother ... I don't know.

HINDL You don't know? How long has it been?

ROKHL Last night. But his kisses mingled with his tears.

HINDL Don't worry, dear. Try not to. With God's help—everything will be alright. Take Yekhezkele and go to sleep now. It's late. Your father will be getting up soon to recite *Khatzois*.

ROKHL — But Doviyd's still not home …

HINDL — Such a bright child. What a little rascal! Sleep now. I'll wait up for Doviyd.

ROKHL — He won't eat if I'm not here. *(Picks up YEKHEZKL and exits with him)*

HINDL — Just like your father. He was the same way when he was younger. He'd come home, sit down and wait for me to attend to him. Men!

DOVIYD, 21 yrs old, enters. He is dressed modestly and not exactly fashionably.

DOVIYD — Good evening.

HINDL — Good morning. Glad you decided to finally come home. Off to bed with me. Your supper's already cold. Go wash your hands. You know—when my father was head of the seminary, he'd send the young men home right after the evening prayers. To their wives.

DOVIYD — Where is Rokhele?

HINDL — In bed. I told her to go. Go ahead. Wash your hands.

DOVIYD — I'm not hungry.

DOVIYD exits.

HINDL — A good sign. A good sign.

HINDL exits. Pause.

HINDL — *(From offstage, praying)* Dear God, let my eyes fall asleep …

VOICE 1 — *(Echoing HINDL in Hebrew) Borrukh ato adoshem, Elokeynu melekh haolam, hamapil khevley shina al eynoy usnuma al afapoy. umeyir l'ishon bas oyin....*

DOVIYD reenters. He sits down at the table, takes up a religious text and begins to mumble the text. ROKHL enters.

ROKHL — Doviyd—

DOVIYD — I thought you'd gone to bed.

ROKHL — Can't sleep.

DOVIYD — How come?

ROKHL — The ice floes on the river are breaking. Can't you hear it? It's deafening to me ...

DOVIYD — First day of Spring was this last Saturday. The river knows it's time to throw off its blanket. Time to move out into the world.

ROKHL — I called you—but you didn't answer. I thought you'd left.

DOVIYD — Why were you scared? You knew I was here. Go back to bed, Rokhele.

ROKHL — Come with me.

DOVIYD — I'll be right in. I'm almost done here. Just need to look something up ... *(Leads her to the door)* Is Yekhezkele asleep?

ROKHL — Finally. It'd be a shame to wake him. Such rosy cheeks. When he smiles, I swear—it's as if he's still learning the secrets of the world from the angels.

ROKHL exits. DOVIYD begins to pace around the room restlessly. He goes to the bookcase, reaches behind the books and takes out a few items of clothing and some books. He starts toward ROKHL's room as she enters from the same direction.

ROKHL Don't lie to me anymore.

DOVIYD What?

ROKHL I know what you're planning to do. God only knows where you're going. God only knows. Last night—last night, when you finally came to bed, I heard everything. Everything.

DOVIYD What? What did you hear, Rokhele?

ROKHL You thought I was asleep. When you lay down next to me … You didn't say anything. You just looked at me—like you wanted to ask me something. I was awake. I didn't want to startle you. I whispered your name. But you didn't hear … You just leaned over and said something. I couldn't hear what you said.

DOVIYD It was nothing.

ROKHL Seemed like you were saying goodbye. Were you? When I opened my eyes, you were standing over our son's crib … You looked at him, you said something to him. Lord knows what.

They are silent.

ROKHL What are you hiding from me? You never talk to me anymore; you avoid me whenever you can. What are you keeping from me—your wife? Your own wife! It's like you're crying inside all the time now. This morning, I heard you studying your texts. I'd never heard your voice sound so sad before. You study to forget now. Drive away your sad thoughts. To forget. And when you do manage to forget—your voice becomes so bright! But then it grows sad again. Dear God—it feels awful. I felt awful. I know you're trying to tell me something, something you can't put into words. You're trying to tell me something through the melodies. I can hear it. And I'm trying—I'm trying to understand you, but I can't. I'm stupid, Doviyd. I can't understand you anymore …

DOVIYD I need to get away, Rokhele.

ROKHL Where? To see your parents?

DOVIYD Away from everyone.

ROKHL Is it so terrible here? With us?

DOVIYD I have everything I need. Everything—and nothing. I don't have anything I need.

ROKHL … Is it me?

DOVIYD No—no, Rokhele. Please understand. I can't stay here. I have to go.

ROKHL This isn't you. Talking like this. This isn't like you at all.

DOVIYD I have everything I need. But I'm suffocating. Look at all these holy books. Big ones. Small ones. They're all shackles around my neck! I want to free myself from these shackles. Can't you understand that? People here are like ghosts to me now. They're born lifeless, their existence is lifeless—and they die lifeless. Generation to generation. Father passes it on to son and then that son passes it on to his, and on and on and on … As soon as our baby opened his eyes, we shackled him. There's no sunshine in his life. No laughter. No life beyond our windows. We keep him ignorant—just so he'll stay here. Amongst all the dusty books. And for what? What hope am I handing our child? I have to go into the world and find a path for myself—for my child—so that he can have a better life than this. *(Beat)* I need your help, Rokhele. Please. For him, for our child—I need to find a new path.

ROKHL This doesn't sound like you. This doesn't sound like you at all ... You've never talked to me like this before, Doviyd.

DOVIYD Something inside me is finally coming alive! I have to follow it. Like the river, I just have to go—I have to go away so I can come back to you. My child will not grow up in this bleakness. Like we did. I need to find a purpose in life. Something to hope for, Rokhele. I need my child to know that there's something out there for him ... Something to pray to. I want to create a bible. I want to create a god for my child.

ROKHL A new god?

DOVIYD Not a new god, Rokhele—a living god.

ROKHL You serve the only living God there is. You've devoted yourself to this God, to please this God. All I've ever wanted was to hear our son praying by your side. He'll follow in your footsteps, you'll see. You'll see. God will help us.

DOVIYD ... I'm a stranger to those who should know me.

ROKHL You'll see. God will help us. Forget all of this. Study Torah with Yekhezkele.

DOVIYD There's another world out there and I can't find a way to get to it.

ROKHL Remember when we were first engaged? I used to stand by the door and listen to you chant. Your voice sang ... It sounded so full. I felt like you were speaking to me. Just to me. Do that again, Doviyd. For me. Please. Forget about all this. Please.

DOVIYD Those who sleep, sing a quiet song; when they awake, the song is interrupted.

VOICE 2 *(Echoing DOVIYD in Hebrew) Eylu ha-yesheyniym, Shariym shiyr kheresh; keshehem ne-oriym, shiyram mufsak.*

ROKHL — Take refuge in me. In my body … I'll make you forget all this, you'll see. Wash it all away. *(YEKHEZKL's voice from the other room calls "Mame,Mame")* Hear that, Doviyd? Can you? That's our child. He has your voice. He's calling out "*Mame*" in your voice. With God's help, he'll sit and study Torah with you, just like you did … *(She exits)*

DOVIYD — Yes. Then his voice will change. It will become sad. It will yearn for something more. Generation after generation … Nothing but empty words.

ROKHL — *(To YEKHEZKL)* Your father's gone very far away. He's climbed up mountains and descended into valleys. Looking for enlightenment. For you, Yekhezkele. To bring you. Your father wants to live among the enlightened—but your mother must stay here in darkness. And where will you live? Your mother must remain here in this place of darkness. But there, in the distance—she'll see a ray of light. That's the land of the enlightened. That's where your father will be, surrounded by light. He'll find a black ray reaching for him from this land of darkness—while you, my darling, you'll stand at the border between us and you won't know which way to turn.

A long pause.

VOICE 2 — *Shema Yisroyl adonyi elokaynew adonay ekhod.*

VOICE 1 — *(Echoing Hebrew of VOICE 2)* Hear O Israel. The lord is our God, there is one lord.

DOVIYD — *(From off stage)* Let me go … *(Pause)* Forget all this. Go to sleep …

Silence.

ROKHL — *(From off stage)* Come back, Doviyd! *(Pause)* Come back!

We hear footsteps. A door opens and closes. A long pause.

VOICE 2 *(From off stage repeats this line over and over, progressively fainter until it disappears) Shteyt uf, shteyt uf. Yiydelekh. Koshere Yiydelekh, frume Yiydelekh, steht uf, steht uf. lavoydas haboy'rey.*

VOICE 1 *(From off stage, echoing Voice 2)* Wake up, wake up. People, dear people, faithful people. Wake up to do God's work.

Pause.

ZOREKH *(Reading aloud from the prayer book)* "By the rivers of Babylon, we sat and wept when we remembered Zion. On the willow trees, we hung harps. Then our tormenters demanded that we sing to them. Sing to us of Zion's songs. How can we sing God's songs on foreign soil? If I should forget you, O Jerusalem, let my right hand forget its powers. Let my tongue cleave to my gums if I don't put Jerusalem before my happiness …"

VOICE 2 *(Echoing ZOREKH) Al naharowt' Ba'vel, sheym yashav'nu gam bakhiy'nu, bezakhrey'nu es Tsiyon. Al araviym' betowkha' taliynu kiynowrowseynu. Kiy shamsheylo'nu shovey'nu diyv'rey shiyr vitolaley'nu siymkha' shiyru' la'nu miy shiyr' Tsiyon' …*

The door is thrust open and we see ROKHL restraining DOVIYD.

DOVIYD *(To ROKHL)* Let go of me! (*To ZOREKH*) Sir!

ZOREKH *(Continues praying)* Foreigners came into your land and made your holy temple impure.

VOICE 2 *(Echoing ZOREKH in Hebrew) Bow'u goyim benakhlose'kho tim'u es eychal kodshe'kho*

DOVIYD Please, sir. I must speak with you …

ZOREKH What is it, Doviyd?

DOVIYD I've decided to leave.

ZOREKH I beg your pardon?

DOVIYD I don't belong here. Not anymore.

ZOREKH What are you saying?

DOVIYD The Torah doesn't speak to me anymore. I have to find another Torah.

ZOREKH What is this? Listen to yourself …

DOVIYD Nothing here has meaning for me anymore! Your Torah is spent! It has no melody … And yet you still sing it? Your Torah is for you, for an ancient people. People sapped of life. Where is a Torah for the young? Will you keep on teaching lessons that have no relevance to life today? When far more relevant lessons are available to us?

ZOREKH My ears must be deceiving me. These aren't your words.

DOVIYD These books! I've become a prisoner of these books. My spirit's been suffocated by them. These books have alienated me from the world right outside our windows … There was laughter coming from the forest and I was drawn to it but you concealed all this from me. You forced me to live here amongst these decaying, dusty books. And I did! I lived here … Never stopping. Even when I stopped believing in this, all of this, I kept chanting lines from the Talmud—so I'd forget. Forget where I was. But I couldn't. I couldn't bury my life. This life in me … Neither can you. Ask the river and it will tell you. You can't bury a life. I've stood by that river for hours—talking to it, asking it to carry my words into the world.

ZOREKH Go wherever you like. You think our God needs people like you? We've survived this long without you—we don't need you now.

DOVIYD I'm not leaving in shame. I'm not leaving in secret, as if I've done something wrong. I leave with a clear conscience. I'm strong enough to leave now … My eyes have been opened. I see how bleak your world is. This is what I'm leaving. There's a world out there for me. I'm leaving to find a god and a torah.

ZOREKH Go—go ahead. Go find a god and lose that god all over again. You'll find another one soon enough … And another once you lose that one, too. You'll change gods like you change your shirts. But know this—you won't remain loyal to any one of them. Not one.

DOVIYD This god will be my soul. My inner self. You don't replace your soul. Your self.

ZOREKH You've lost your self! Try all you want—but you'll fail. You'll deceive yourself along with the rest of the world …

DOVIYD No—

ZOREKH Your compass is lost. You'll wander blindly, searching for this God. You'll pray to something, anything—even when there's nothing to believe in any longer. You'll search for Gods, supplanting them with others when you find one that feels better. Shopping for a God. You'll latch on to each one, diluting their teachings more and more, long after you've stopped believing in them … You'll serve every God—but none of them will be yours. None of them. You'll wander from one country to another, but you won't feel at home anywhere. You'll mouth the words of every language, but none of them will be your *mameloshen.* You'll become nothing but a traveling salesman, selling beliefs door to door.

DOVIYD I need something to believe in …

ZOREKH You won't find it here.

ROKHL enters with the child in her arms.

ROKHL Doviyd!

ZOREKH Your husband's dead.

DOVIYD exits.

ZOREKH You are a widow now. Let me tear your dress for you. *(He cuts her dress, the child's shirt, and the lapel of his coat)* Now you can sit *shiyva* for your husband.

HINDL enters.

HINDL What's happened?

ZOREKH *(Takes the prayerbook and recites)* "Remember what has become of us, God. Behold our shame. Our children have gone into the hands of strangers."

VOICE 2 *(Echoing ZOREKH in Hebrew) Z'khor adoshem meh hoyo lonu habita u'r'ey es kherposeynu. nakhaloseynu nehepkho l'zorim boteynu l'nokhrim. somim hoyinuv'eyn ov imoseynu k'almones.*

Act Two

Five years later. It is winter. ZOREKH sits at a table over an open Talmud. HINDL is reading in a chair. There is a bowl of apples on the table. ZOREKH and HINDL freeze as a spotlight comes up on DOVIYD, looking very chic, elegant, hip.

DOVIYD

The river led me to the city, as if its currents were dragging me along. I felt like flotsam, nothing but debris drifting without direction. Without purpose. But there was a pull—a gravity that drew me towards light, towards sound. The sound of … laughter. Women's laughter. All in unison, as if in a chorus. The city streets were full of it. Never had I heard such happiness before. A happiness that seems to come from somewhere else, somewhere I'd never found it before—not from the soul, but from the back of the throat. The lips. The teeth. A happiness that adds color to ones cheek, letting the blood flow full and ruddy. As if to dip oneself into a fine red wine. Let it soak into your skin. I followed that laughter as deep as I could, nearly diving down these women's throats. Drowning in their mouths. Taking them into my lungs. The perfumes. The meats. Fattening myself on laughter. On food. On spirits—letting them possess me, one glass at a time. I could never drink enough, never eat enough. If I had an inch left within my belly, I'd fill it. A centimeter. A millimeter.

No amount of emptiness need be left within me—I wanted to be full, full of all this. If this laughter could have swallowed me in return, I would've let it, let it devour me whole—because it eased the flow of my own blood, like a flood in my own veins, never had I felt the blood course through my body with such a surge … And if I woke without that feeling within me, I'd find it again. And if that feeling ever drifted off during the day, I'd moor myself to it however I could. Through spirits. Through women. Through food. Through laughter. Until there was nothing of me beyond it. Empty guffaws. Shallow laughter, until it sounded as if that laughter had turned. Now it sounded like everyone was laughing at me …

Lights shift. Spotlight fades to black. A second spotlight up on ROKHL on opposite side of the stage.

ROKHL

There's this dream that follows me through my sleep. I'm standing upon the river, feet planted on the ice. It can only be a few inches thick. I know how dangerous this is—but I have to find him, I know he's out there somewhere on the river. And then … I hear a crack from beneath me. The ice at my feet begins to break away. Then another. The whole river fractures off into dozens of shards. I'm standing upon a piece of ice no bigger than my body, struggling to keep my balance as it drifts down the river. My own little iceberg. There's no way of stepping off. I can't jump, forced to stand in place on this sliver of ice as it floats downriver. It strikes another piece of ice, and another small section falls off. It happens again—another section breaking away. I have to stand directly in the center for fear of slipping into the cold water surrounding me. The further downriver my iceberg goes, the smaller it becomes—until there's nothing but the ice directly beneath my feet. Mere inches. From my toes to my heels. Nothing more. And then, before long, there isn't even enough ice for my feet to rest upon. I have to stand on the tips of my toes. I begin to lose my balance. If I lean over too far to one side, my iceberg begins to wobble ... So I call out Doviyd's name. I haven't said his name out loud for so long. Hearing me say it, his name from my own voice ... It sounds strange even to me. I can see my breath fog up before my face—as if his very name were freezing within the air. No warmth to it at all. His name's the last thing to come out from my mouth before I fall into the stinging water. Rather than take the air into my lungs one last time before plunging under the surface, I choose to utter his name one last time. I say his name—and then what air's left in my lungs freezes over. And just as I feel that coldness swallow me, I wake up. Shivering to the bone. *(Beat)* This is when I know—in my heart, I know—that Doviyd is gone.

Spotlight goes off abruptly. ROKHL exits. DOVIYD has already disappeared. ZOREKH and HINDL unfreeze.

HINDL: Oh God—what should I do? He thinks this has nothing to do with him. Her predicament never crosses his mind ...

ZOREKH: Are you speaking to me, Hindl?

HINDL: Hard to say.

ZOREKH: What's gotten into you?

HINDL: Go ahead—ignore everything. There's your Talmud. Nothing else matters. A cloud hangs over our daughter and you could care less. Five years now, she's been in this state. Five long years.

ZOREKH: What am I to do?

HINDL: What should you do?

ZOREKH: Tell me—what I am supposed to do?

HINDL Men have it so easy. God gave you the Talmud. If something bothers you, you just lose yourself in the Talmud. Always the Talmud! But what about women? How are we supposed to cope? There she is—26 years old and she'll never remarry. The best years of her life—all lost. Zorekh—a father can't understand it like a mother can. She won't say a word about it. She's too shy for that. But her eyes! Her eyes speak volumes to me … She needs a man.

ZOREKH A man!

HINDL It means so little to you. But she is a woman—

ZOREKH You believe she still thinks about him?

HINDL She yearns for him!

ZOREKH How do you know? She never talks about Doviyd …

HINDL Don't mention his name! Not when she's around. Ever since Eliezer told her he saw him in the city with those women … You can see it in her eyes. The mere mention of his name and she pales! She still hungers for him … she needs a man.

ZOREKH Dear God.

HINDL Just like that—she'll start crying! Breaks my heart. The tears are for him … For him! It means nothing to you—a young woman, spending her days staring out the window for hours. Watching other young women parade down the street, all dressed up. Beaming … Each one has her own home, a husband. And Rokhele. Alone. And this means nothing to you …

ZOREKH We've done our part. I've said what a father should say. What more can I do?

HINDL But what's going to happen to her? Day after day. Weeks fly by and she simply sits there …

ZOREKH Hindl, I'm going to the synagogue. Tell Rokhele to meet me after the services. Tell her I want to talk to her.

ZOREKH exits.

HINDL (*Calling offstage*) Yekhezkele! Time to go back to school. It's getting dark.

HINDL exits. ROKHL enters with YEKHEZKL, now a small boy.

YEKHEZKL No, *Mame*!

ROKHL You'll freeze! It's cold outside …

YEKHEZKL No, *Mame*—it's not cold at all.

ROKHL Silly boy … Listen to your *mame* and you won't get sick. Then you'll have the strength to study the Torah.

YEKHEZKL But we started a new lesson—and I already know it better than anybody else. Want to hear it, *Mame*?

ROKHL Your *mame* loves you so much! (*Kisses him*)

YEKHEZKL (*Wipes the kiss away.*) Don't you want to hear it, *Mame*? (*He goes to the bookcase*) Where's the *Bava mstsiye*? Here it is. Okay … Hold on. (*Opens the book and recites aloud*) "Two people are fighting over a cloak. One says I found it and the other says I found it. What should they do? The law says: It must be divided …"

VOICE 2 *Shnay'im okhaz'in bita'lis: ze omer aniy' mitzosi'ho vize' omer aniy' mitzosi'ho. viha'din: yachlo'ku.*

ROKHL His voice … His voice must have sounded like that as a child. It sounded like that when we got married. Where are you? Come back, Doviyd. Do you hear that? Your child is chanting Talmud …

YEKHEZKL Who are you talking to, *Mame*?

ROKHL No one, *mayn eytzer*. (*She kisses him*)

YEKHEZKL (*Rubbing off her kiss*) My teacher says you're not allowed to let any woman kiss you …

ROKHL *(Kissing him)* Silly boy ... A *mame*'s not just any woman. I'm your *mame*! A *mame*'s allowed ...

YEKHEZKL Not even my *mame*!

HINDL enters.

HINDL Run along, Yekhezkele. It's late. Back to school ...

YEKHEZKL My teacher told us to bring money for supplies—

HINDL *(Searches her purse)* Those teachers ... *(Hands him some money)*

YEKHEZKL And can I buy a snack?

HINDL *(Gives him more money)* Okay ... Now go!

ROKHL Wait ...

ROKHL hands him an apple from the bowl on the table.

HINDL Go, go! Walk on the sidewalk so you don't get run over! Hear me? Don't you dare play on the ice. And don't give your snack away to your friends, okay?

YEKHEZKL *(Biting into the apple)* Alright, alright!

HINDL Did you say the blessing for the apple?

YEKHEZKL I did ...

HINDL Let's go ...

YEKHEZKL exits, followed by HINDL.

ROKHL My precious child ... The river is finally beginning to quiet down. Tucked under a hard white blanket of snow. It's rocking more gently. Wind lulls it to sleep, wraps it in a white shroud. It will be still soon. It will stop racing ... and finally it'll sleep peacefully under the ice. But I can still hear it rushing. The river rocking so fiercely! Racing from one end of the world to the other.

Its ice covering breaks. Delicate panes of glass shattering. Icy winds stirring up the snow—it's quieting down. Trembling slightly … Shhhh. Now the river goes back to sleep. The wind sings its lullaby …

HINDL reenters.

HINDL — It's cold. Going to be a bad winter … I pity the poor. *(She bangs on the wall) Khane, Khane*! Let's have some heat! The radiator's cold. Rokhele, don't stand by the window! You'll get sick …

Long pause. We hear the Kedusha prayer being recited. HINDL rises, faces east and quietly responds to it.

ROKHL — Why does Father want to see me?

HINDL — He wants to talk to you. God makes everything right if he chooses to. Everything is in God's hands. Oh, Rokhele … Rokhele—you wouldn't do anything foolish, would you? Please talk to me?

ROKHL — What do you want me to say?

HINDL — You have nothing to tell me?

ROKHL — What do you want me to say?

HINDL — You think I don't understand, don't you? You won't talk to me. That hurts. You behave as if there is no God to help you, as if … he's the only man on earth.

ROKHL — Please—don't.

HINDL — Rokhele … You won't do anything rash, will you? Today I read that King Soloman once wanted to test God. He snatched a girl from her mother and placed her in a glass house in a remote desert where no one had ever set foot … He found a bird to bring her food from the King's table. And what did God do? He created a storm at sea, battering a ship that carried the man who was destined to be her husband. That man held fast to a piece of wreckage and the wind steered him right to her island ... All doors have yet to be closed. God makes anything possible.

ROKHL I've already found my soul mate. And I lost him ...

HINDL You still think about him, don't you?

ROKHL Mother ... I don't know.

HINDL Thank goodness.

ZOREKH enters.

ZOREKH Hindl—let's have some light.

HINDL You're here. Good. *(Turns on the light)* I can't handle this.

HINDL exits. ROKHL begins to follow her out.

ZOREKH Rokhele ...

ROKHL What?

ZOREKH Sit down—please. I want to talk to you. You've been avoiding me, haven't you? *(No reply)* I know you're angry with me. Do you honestly think that your father is so ...

ROKHL What makes you say that?

ZOREKH Do you really think I don't suffer along with you? You're my child! And not just with you—with him. He was also my child.

ROKHL Daddy ...

ZOREKH The Talmud says: He who teaches someone torah, it's as if he gave him life itself.

VOICE 2 *(Echoing ZOREKH in Hebrew) Kohl hamlamed es ben khaveyro toyre kiiylu yoldo.*

ZOREKH I taught Doviyd.

ROKHL Don't say his name—please! I can't bear it.

ZOREKH I had high hopes for him. I honestly believed he would carry the torch of the Torah forward.

ROKHL Daddy, please—stop....

ZOREKH You must realize that no one is to blame. Not I, not you. Not even Doviyd.

ROKHL Daddy ...

ZOREKH Do you understand? Not even Doviyd is to blame! He began to reflect, to question ... But God demands faith! Faith comes from the heart—not the mind. There are plenty of questions, certainly. Of course! But as Jews, we must fulfill our obligations. No matter what, at any cost. That's what makes us Jews. Whoever strays from the path of the Jewish people is no longer one of us ...

VOICE 2 *(Echoing ZOREKH's last line in Hebrew) kohl ha sote miy darkoh shel ha am ha yehudiy, loh ohd ekhud meytanu hu*

ZOREKH That is what makes us Jews.

ROKHL What'll I tell Yekhezkele? When he asks me where his father is, what should I say? All the other children at school have fathers. He's the only one ... Living or dead, he has nothing!

ZOREKH Tell him the truth. Tell him his father left and you don't know where ...

ROKHL But I do know! In my heart, I know!

ZOREKH When he's older, he'll understand. But that's not what I wanted to talk about. Rokhele ... Tell me honestly. Do you still love Doviyd? *(Pause)* I know he is your husband. It can't be easy. You were close. And don't just tell me what I want to hear. You're letting your life waste away ... Look at yourself. Look deep inside yourself. Can you go on without him?

ROKHL ... I don't know.

ZOREKH Even after what Eliezer told you?

ROKHL I don't know …

There is a knock at the door.

ZOREKH Who is it?

Pause. ROKHL opens the door. DOVIYD enters. ROKHL does not recognize him.

DOVIYD Rokhele!

ROKHL Mother! Mother!

ROKHL exits.

ZOREKH Doviyd?

DOVIYD Yes.

ZOREKH Why have you come? To see your wife and child?

DOVIYD I've come to see you too.

ZOREKH What do you mean—me? Haven't you found your path?

DOVIYD When you lose your way, you don't find another.

HINDL enters.

HINDL Doviyd … Is that you? Doviyd!

ZOREKH Hindl, we have things to discuss.

HINDL It's Doviyd. It's Doviyd!

HINDL exits.

ZOREKH Why have you come to see me?

DOVIYD Not just to see you. To see everything. Everything I lost. Here, among these books … You can only believe once. I went out into the world, I tore my soul to shreds. I gave each shred another label. Labels … In place of beliefs. I cashed in beliefs for labels and everyone understood that currency … Everybody deals in labels. But that's not why I'm here … It's all over. I can't lull myself to sleep with your Talmudic melody anymore. Everything, everything in this house … I destroyed myself.

ZOREKH Then why are you here?

DOVIYD I came for my wife and child.

ZOREKH You've come for Yekhezkele? What kind of faith can you offer him?

DOVIYD I don't have to give him faith. I'll teach him what I know. He can discover the rest for himself.

ZOREKH No—we won't allow it. We are Jews. My daughter is a Jewish woman. She won't go with you!

DOVIYD We'll see—

ZOREKH She gave up on you! You betrayed her! She doesn't want to know you! She won't go …

DOVIYD *(Calls to ROHKELE off stage)* Rokhele … I've come back. For you. I'm here for you.

ZOREKH She's not answering you.

DOVIYD *(Still to ROKHL offstage)* Should I leave? Your husband has come for you …

ROKHL enters.

DOVIYD Sir. This is between me and my wife—

ZOREKH She may be your wife—but I am a Jew, and I will not allow a Jewish soul to fall into impure hands!

DOVIYD *(To ROKHL)* Choose, then. Your father or me. Here your life will be easy. You'll ape our ancestors. One generation after another of Jewish faith … I can't give you that. I went out into the world to search for God. I found nothing … I searched in book after book for what I'd lost in these books. I studied. I believed, I joyously believed what I was studying …

ROKHL Doviyd?

DOVIYD I saw you in the distance, sitting with my son. You were waiting for me and it gave me such strength. I believed in that one moment … But then, I don't know. I no longer saw you. You were not with me anymore. You no longer believed in me. You abandoned me. I stopped believing in myself or anything around me. Everything seemed so small … Why? I asked myself. Why dig and search? Life is too short to spend looking for a purpose. I'm tired. I just wanted to lay my head in your lap. I wanted you to sing me to sleep. I wanted to forget everything! The only thing I still believed in was your love … I want to find my life in that love again. Please. Won't you come with me, Rokhele?

ROKHL You've been gone for far too long … I don't know you anymore, Doviyd. Something of you died inside me. There's the scent of another woman on your body. Someone else's hair has been between your fingers. You've been away for too long. Far too long. Something of you died in me.

ZOREKH Oh, my Rokhele …

DOVIYD starts to leave.

ROKHL No! I love you! Take me … Take me with you. I love you just the way you are … Dance with other women, if you must … Kiss them. I love you! I am going with you.

ZOREKH What about God?!

ROKHL God can punish me. I love him … I have to go with him.

ZOREKH And the child, Rokhele? What about the child?

ROKHL *(To DOVIYD)* I am yours. My soul is in your hands. Do whatever you want with me—but I'm not giving you my child … He is a Jew.

ZOREKH Thank God!

YEKHEZKL *(From offstage) Mame, Mame* my teacher said I know the lesson better than … *(He enters and sees the stranger who is DOVIYD)*

ROKHL This is your father, Yekhezkele.

YEKHEZKL I don't want him for a father.

DOVIYD He'll come on his own.

CURTAIN

Moshke Khazer or Under the Cross (Untern Tzeylm)

By I.D. Berkowitz

Translation from Yiddish by Mark Altman, Ellen Perecman and Baruch Thaler

Adaptation by Mark Altman, Ellen Perecman and Clay McLeod Chapman

Characters

MOSHKE FEROPONTOV	A Jewish convert to Christianity
AVDOTYE	His wife
YAKOV	Their son
TANYE	Yakov's wife
KIYRL KIRILITSH PYATAK	A former deacon
HAVRILO	Employee of Moshke
ALYOSHKE	Havrila's son, a hunchback, also employed by Moshke
MEYER BER	An urban Jew
ROKHTCHE	His daughter
AKIM	A peasant gang leader
TOWNSPEOPLE	

Act One

Just before sundown on Yom Kippur eve. Moshke's house. A large bright room with windows that look out on an enclosed garden. There is a small religious icon on a shelf.

AVDOTYE is spinning wool. TANYE sits at the table reading a book.

AVDOTYE — It's getting dark. He hasn't even rounded up the cows yet … Still drizzling. Winter's on its way. (To TANYE.) Why don't you go outside and see where he is, that useless hunchback? Time to milk the cows. *(Pause)* Tanye, Tanye!

TANYE — Did you say something?

AVDOTYE — I said: it's time to milk the cows. And you just sit there, deep in thought … We can't have that, my dear!

TANYE — Can't have … what?

AVDOTYE — Getting lost in your thoughts. Always reading …

TANYE — Am I bothering anyone?

AVDOTYE — It bothers me. You glued to that book!

TANYE — Why should it? There might not be much of a life for me here—but at least I can read about the lives of others … It's not that late. Let the cows graze a little longer.

AVDOTYE Times like these, you can't leave cows alone for long. People have become desperate ... And how did he buy all this stuff anyway? *(Points to the breakfront)* Gold, watches, expensive jewelry—now I can understand all that. They've become more valuable than money. But books? Scribbled pages? They aren't good for anything but blowing your nose!

TANYE Forgive me—but what an ignorant thing to say!

AVDOTYE I say ignorant things because I am ignorant! And who are you to insult me, Tanike? I feed you—not the other way around.

TANYE I'm not accustomed to having people talk to me like this ...

AVDOTYE Get accustomed to it. When you live among wolves, you howl like wolves ... Understand?

TANYE When I lived with my uncle's family, no one ever talked about taking care of me as a burden. It's been a year. And life here hasn't exactly been a bed of roses ... so why are you bringing this up now?

AVDOTYE I didn't mean anything by it, silly child. Forget it. *(Under her breath)* Shouldn't aggravate your husband like that ...

TANYE I aggravate him?

AVDOTYE He doesn't want you to be a ... a fine young lady who reads books. You do as he says!

TANYE When Moshke came to see my uncle about arranging this marriage, he told him: "I want her in my family because she is refined."

AVDOTYE That was your father-in-law. This is your husband. The husband is the master. You respect him.

TANYE Respect him! Is it okay that he goes out dancing all night with other girls? He gropes girls, and they laugh in my face—does that meet with your approval?

AVDOTYE So what if my son likes a casual caress against a girl? That's normal for peasant boys …

TANYE I didn't know I was marrying a peasant …

AVDOTYE Don't insult your husband, Tanika!

TANYE I come from a respectable family. My father didn't grope girls in public. He wasn't vulgar.

AVDOTYE Why don't you ask me how I treated my husband when we were younger!

TANYE Your husband is different. He's respectable …

AVDOTYE He sure is! Quite a head on his shoulders! But remember where he comes from.

TANYE Our God, the Lord, also descended from Jews.

AVDOTYE Cross yourself, you foolish girl! *(AVDOTYE crosses herself)*

TANYE That's what it says in the Holy Scriptures.

AVDOTYE I was taught that the Scriptures say the very opposite: the Jews tortured Jesus!

TANYE They tortured him because he was one of their own … Ask your husband, he'll tell you the same thing!

AVDOTYE Ask him about such things? God forbid!

TANYE Are you going to wax poetic about when you were young?

AVDOTYE My dear, it's a very long story. I'm not sure I'd even know how to tell you … The first time I met him I was afraid of him!

TANYE Afraid? Why?

AVDOTYE He's a Jew …

TANYE But he converted!

AVDOTYE Converted, yes. The holy water purified him. But there's still evil inside him. May the Good Lord not punish me … *(Crosses herself)* Believe me, I've often felt a tightness right here, near my heart … I was drawn to him, like being pulled by a rope!

TANYE It sounds like you really loved him.

AVDOTYE How could you not? There was no one like him.

TANYE Was he handsome?

AVDOTYE Handsome, tall. Smart. Just out of the army—and he sure was different!

TANYE Still is … Why did he leave his own community?

AVDOTYE I can't tell you for sure. Either because those devils drove him away, or because he saw the true light …

TANYE How did you two meet?

AVDOTYE God led him to good people. We are of refined stock, even if we never opened a book. My father, may he rest in paradise, was the wealthiest Kolbasa merchant in town.

TANYE And you?

AVDOTYE Me? I was a girl. With delicate skin. I was a delight, like any young girl raised in the country. Healthy, too. Not like these pale Jewish women …

TANYE And after the wedding? Things went well?

AVDOTYE Oh, not well! Not well, dear! How could it have, when the devil still hadn't been smoked out of him? He came from them. He never belonged here with us … He had sinned against God. Went to church every Sunday, but at home, when no one was watching … he would sling mud.

TANYE Who did he sling it at?

AVDOTYE Everyone! He mocked anything that was holy. At night, dear, he didn't cross himself before going to bed …

TANYE Maybe he thought about slinking back to his old life?

AVDOTYE No—he hated them more than us. If one of them ever got lost and stumbled into our yard, he'd throw sticks at them ...

TANYE Rumor has it that the Jews have a name for him: Moshke *Khazer* ...

AVDOTYE Not so loud! He'll be back any minute ... If he hears someone use that name, he'll kill him! He once broke one of their boys' legs for using it. That mangy little dog was chasing him and yelling—so he caught him, broke his leg. Crippled him forever ... That's why we moved out here. He said, "I don't want to look at their scabby faces anymore."

TANYE Jews aren't allowed to eat pork. I hear it disgusts them.

AVDOTYE And you think it doesn't disgust him? First time he was offered pork he couldn't even look at it. My father, may he rest in paradise, was a sausage-maker. Always having pork. But my husband wouldn't eat it. "Why don't you eat it?" I asked. "Because," he said, "it stinks." So I went to the Jewish shoemaker in town and asked her to teach me how to cook their dishes, may the Lord not punish me for it ...

TANYE Did you learn?

AVDOTYE *Kugel, tsiymes, kiyshke*. May God not punish me ... *(She crosses herself again)* Even then, though—he didn't like the way I prepared them. So he got used to pork ...

TANYE Really? How fascinating!

AVDOTYE Fascinating for you. For me, my dear, it's a sin! Your husband is your master, second only to God. But you think that was all? *(Whispers)* He didn't want to have any children!

TANYE No children? Why on earth not?

AVDOTYE Who knows? People's souls are a mystery. Certainly true of him ...

TANYE But … you had a child.

AVDOTYE God arranged that too. And I sure suffered for it! When he found out I was pregnant, he left. Didn't return for three days!

TANYE Then what?

AVDOTYE He wouldn't speak to me at all after that. I'd have to sit alone and swallow my tears … That's why Yakov was born so sad.

TANYE So that's why he doesn't love Yakov …

AVDOTYE Doesn't love him? Oh no. After he was born, he'd cuddle with him whenever I wasn't looking … See how stingy he is with every penny? Well … When Yashenka was sick once, he ran off to the city in middle of the night, bringing back the best doctor. Paid him twenty-five rubles for the visit.

TANYE He once told me that if Yasha wanted to be cultured, he'd spend every penny he had on him.

AVDOTYE He was adamant—he wanted his child to read and write. He'd torment him, drive him to distraction. He once nearly whipped him … And the child was so stubborn! He didn't want to learn! Always wanting to be like all the other Christian children. How they quarrel! They've been arguing as long as I can remember. Lord only knows the vicious cycle this will lead to …

TANYE Yasha would have been much better off if he'd been educated …

AVDOTYE How? How would he have been better off?

TANYE Our world's been liberated. The lower classes are a higher status now. We should have moved to the city, our lives would have been so much better …

AVDOTYE This village isn't good enough for you?

TANYE How can you live here? You can't light a lamp for fear you'll be attacked!

AVDOTYE That's why there's enough to eat in the village. And in the city? In the city, people are starving. Dropping like flies! In the city, there's shooting in the streets …

TANYE Yasha went to the city this morning!

AVDOTYE He wanted a pair of boots. His father gave him the money.

TANYE That's not what I heard …

AVDOTYE What did you hear?

TANYE He went to start trouble!

AVDOTYE Trouble? … Where?

TANYE In the towns, where the Jews live …

AVDOTYE Where did you hear that?

TANYE Alyoshke told me. He said a gang armed with axes and scythes had gathered. They were on their way to Murovanke. Yasha is with them …

AVDOTYE All-merciful God! Why did you let him go?

TANYE You think he listens to me?

AVDOTYE Why didn't you tell me?!

TANYE How would it have helped? Someone's coming …

The door opens and PYATAK enters. He is in his 50's. He is dressed in a tattered coat. There is a walking stick in his hand and a faded red army cap on his head. He is drunk.

PYATAK God help the proletariat!

AVDOTYE Well, well! If it isn't Father *Kiril*?

PYATAK It's me, all right.

AVDOTYE It's been a long time! … They said you'd been shot.

PYATAK Shot, dear woman … But not killed! Not enough gunpowder to do me in. *(Notices TANYE)* Ah! I see there's a new face in your house. Your daughter-in-law?

AVDOTYE A city girl.

PYATAK *(Stands at attention)* It's my honor, *Tovarishch*! Kiril Kirilitsh Pyatak, former servant of God—now commissar of the starving people …

AVDOTYE Where did you disappear to?

PYATAK I wandered from city to city, village to village. I observed people ruling the world, now that God has abandoned it … And here, I see, everything is as before: spinning wool, preparing for the winter. The whole world is crumbling, falling to pieces—and only Moshke remains stable! My oldest son, Israel, is not lost … He sends his regards.

AVDOTYE Were you at the mill?

PYATAK I've been everywhere! I even met your husband early this morning on the main road.

AVDOTYE On the main road? All-merciful God! He never goes to Muravanka …

PYATAK And what if he did?

AVDOTYE Didn't you hear? There's going to be trouble in the city today!

PYATAK Oh no—it should be quiet and peaceful. Jews are getting ready for their holy day. Watching them prepare, I felt homesick for my village …

AVDOTYE Did my husband say anything?

PYATAK He was in a foul mood.

AVDOTYE Where did he go?

PYATAK To none other than the house of worship.

AVDOTYE Which?

PYATAK — The Jewish synagogue. To the temple of ancient Jehovah, who still refuses to surrender …

AVDOTYE — What are you blabbering about, Father? I don't understand …

PYATAK — To understand what I say—you have to be learned! Don't you know that today is *Yom Kiypper?* It's no coincidence that there is a wind blowing outside? The rain is whipping up! *Khapun*, the Jewish devil, is at this moment roaming over the empty fields …

AVDOTYE — *(Crosses herself again)* O Lord, be merciful and protect us!

PYATAK — I'll also cross myself … *(Turns to face the icon)* Jews were running off to synagogue … I longed for my village. *(Goes to cross himself but doesn't)* What is this? God's lamp has gone out!

AVDOTYE — Don't blame me, Father. Oil is hard to come by these days.

PYATAK — But there are full barrels of kerosene in the mill! And you, *Krosatke*—you are sitting there all alone? Where is your husband, the young Prince of Judah?

TANYE — I don't know …

PYATAK — He's off to Palestine!

TANYE — Palestine?

PYATAK — To the holy land. That's where all the young Jews are going these days …

AVDOTYE — Someone seems to have had one too many …

PYATAK — I'm drunk, yes. But not from wine, as it says in the Holy Scriptures. Whiskey! Plain old whiskey! *(Takes a bottle of whiskey out of his pocket)* It was a gift given to me by some fine people. *Samogonka*, homemade … Dear woman … Don't you have a piece of bread to munch on? A pickle perhaps?

AVDOTYE Where would I get bread to give you? He says he wants a pickle!

PYATAK Permit me to take a sip … *(Takes a few sips)* Eh! Supplies are running low!

AVDOTYE And you're still sinning, Father, drowning your soul!

PYATAK I don't drink for pleasure, dear woman. I drink from loneliness! We're now in an age of isolation! No more tsar! God's been chased him away! Churches are empty … You wander around alone in this freedom, just like an orphan, and … and you gradually become a drunk … *(Takes another sip and puts away the bottle)*

AVDOTYE And where did you get that hat on your head? Did you join up with the red devils, those bandits?

PYATAK Not bandits, you ignorant woman. Commissars! Rrrrevolutionaries— you hear? (*Takes off the hat)* I inherited this from a commissar who was killed on the main road. *(To TANYE)* And you, *mademoiselle*? Any opinion on the commissars?

TANYE The way I see it, Father … They're the only people maintaining some order in this country.

PYATAK Oh, their order is magnificent! None of the trains move and all the horses are dying … *sha shtil*! You can stagger about in the street like a drunk. No one runs you over! *(To TANYE) Tovarishtch*! Have mercy on a wandering Christian soul! Give me a pickle to nibble on!

AVDOTYE Why are you asking her? This isn't her house!

PYATAK *(To TANYE)* At least give me a piece of paper from your book to roll a cigarette! Tear out a page …

TANYE It's an important book.

PYATAK Who's the author?

TANYE Tolstoy.

PYATAK Oh! The Count? … You're right. To tear up a book of his is a sin! He was a holy man. May he have a bright paradise. He spoke out on God's behalf, sermonizing soberly. But how did his book wind up here in ol' Moshke's house?

AVDOTYE Paid top dollar for it, that's how! Here! Here's a whole bookcase!

PYATAK *(Goes to the bookcase)* Look at this! In my state I didn't even notice it … What are all these gilded chairs? A real throne! I'm impressed. I'm impressed with my eldest son, Israel! And what's this? An entire archive! Fascinating …

PYATAK starts to get up on a stool to reach it. AVDOTYE stops him.

AVDOTYE Don't climb up there with your muddy feet!

TANYE Those are old newspapers. My father-in-law has been saving them for years.

PYATAK Old newspapers! People all over Russia are looking for these! … *(To AVDOTYE)* Allow me, dear woman, to make a requisition. One page for a cigarette … Please. *(Stands on a stool and pulls a page out of one of the bundles)*

AVDOTYE Don't touch! Don't touch! Don't you dare touch them when he's not home!

PYATAK *(Climbs down off the stool)* Alright! Alright! I won't touch! I hold a person's private property sacred. I'll only look at it. It's a long time since I read a newspaper …

AVDOTYE Put it back when you're done!

PYATAK Private property is sacred to me …

PYATAK sits at the table and spreads out the newspaper. ALYOSHKE enters. He is barefoot and holds a whip in his hand.

AVDOTYE Oh, here he is! The hunchback devil! Why so late?

ALYOSHKE I let the cows graze until they got this big! *(Shows with his hands)*

AVDOTYE And milk?

ALYOSHKE What udders!

AVDOTYE Nobody bothered you?

ALYOSHKE Of course they bothered me. So I made a ruckus, luring an officer with his gun.

AVDOTYE You didn't take a swig yourself, did you?

ALYOSHKE May God strike me otherwise!

AVDOTYE *(To PYATAK)* What a time we live in! Neighbors from one village capture your cows in the pasture and milk them dry! … And this hunchback devil here, you think he doesn't do it? He lies down under the cow's udders and sucks on them, like he's drinking from a barrel. I hope leeches suck on this dog! …

ALYOSHKE *(Smiles with embarrassment at PYATAK)* May God strike me down!

AVDOTYE We have a guest—Father Kiril. Go over to him, and he'll bless you.

ALYOSHKE I'd rather you gave me some bread to eat. I can bless myself!

AVDOTYE God didn't put a hump on your shoulders for nothing! Come drive the cows into the stable. *(To TANYE)* And you stay in the house! I'll manage alone.

AVDOTYE winks at TANYE to keep her eye on PYATAK and exits with ALYOSHKE following her.

TANYE *(Runs to the door)* Alyoshke, wait! *(Whispers)* Did they really go?

ALYOSHKE Yup. They left very early. Boys from three villages.

TANYE Are you sure he went with them?

ALYOSHKE They say that he was a little reluctant. Seems as if he was afraid the master might find out. So they started laughing at him, calling him a coward …

TANYE How do you know?

ALYOSHKE Akim's boys. You, miss, shouldn't worry so much. Working over Jews is easy. Easy as spitting! He'll bring you some gifts from the city. Silk handkerchiefs. Akim's boys were bragging that they'll take enough stuff to fill up the house tonight. They said they'd bring along some Jewish girls as well … Lots of fun. If it wasn't for my hump, I'd have gone with them! *(Pause)* Lady … You promised me some cheese.

TANYE Ok … later. Tomorrow.

ALYOSHKE Remember! When I tell the master about this, he'll give me two pieces of cheese!

ALYOSHKE exits.

PYATAK Something's troubling you … What's wrong?

TANYA It's such a confusing time, Father.

PYATAK Oh, what a time, what a time! When I read the newspaper, I feel like I'm dreaming … Once there was a world … Listen to this … *(Reads)* Various colonial merchandise … delicious herring, mixed roe … And further down: Warsaw footwear … the best pair of shoes for four rubles … And I, God's servant, tread barefoot with my aching feet. In the damp. In the cold … *(Looks in the newpaper)* And what is this? Protopopov Brothers Bakery … Dear brothers Protopopov, what's happened to you now? A slice of bread, a white roll to refresh the faint Christian people! …

TANYA Hold on, Father. I'll be right back! *(She exits and returns with bread and a pickle)* Here's some bread, and here's a pickle!

PYATAK A pickle!

TANYA Eat it quickly, before my mother-in-law gets back.

PYATAK My God! A sour pickle! It wasn't a dream, but real! … I can't bring myself to eat it. Better save it. My pickle, my little orphan! How did you survive the great destruction? … *(Rolls it up in the newspaper and puts it inside his coat. Tanya begins to weep)* Why are you crying, child? Me, I cry because I have no strength left …

TANYA I've got so much on my mind, Father …

PYATAK Hard to live with Jews, isn't it? …

AVDOTYA enters with a bucket in her hand.

AVDOTYA What a worthless piece of shit! Didn't I say he would suck the cows dry?! *(Carries the bucket over to TANYA)* Look how much I squeezed out! Look, Father. Be a witness! …

PYATAK looks in the bucket. AVDOTYA makes her way to the door.

AVDOTYA Ah, you stupid hunchback! I hope your belly swells from hunger …

AVDOTYA exits. TANYA also gets up to leave. The door opens slowly and YAKOV appears. He is in his early 20's, blonde. His forehead is wrapped in a blood soaked rag.

TANYA Yasha!

YAKOV Is my father home?

TANYA He's not here ... My God! What happened to you?

YAKOV Where's my mother?

TANYA Here she comes. My God! They shot you? ...

YAKOV turns around and tries to leave as AVDOTYA arrives.

AVDOTYA Yashenka's back? Thank God ... What's this, darling?

YAKOV Get some water and clean linen, fast!

AVDOTYA I'll get the water ... All-merciful God!

AVDOTYA exits.

TANYA I have a piece of clean cottom ...

TANYA exits.

YAKOV I don't need her fucking cotton! Linen! Linen and a towel!

AVDOTYA reenters carrying a bowl.

AVDOTYA Here's some water ... God in heaven, what happened?

YAKOV Stop screaming! Nothing happened. Just clean me up.

YAKOV takes the bloodied rag off his head.

AVDOTYA Where's the cut? I can't see, it's so dark in here.

TANYA reenters.

TANYA Here's some cotton.

YAKOV Why the fuck is she insisting on cotton? Turn some light on!

AVDOTYA Turn on the light.

TANYA I am!

AVDOTYA Now I can see. There's a cut here on his forehead.

YAKOV Is it deep?

AVDOTYA No, I don't think so … Your face is just covered with blood.

YAKOV Wash it off, fast! He may be back any minute now …

TANYA Here's a clean towel.

AVDOTYA Bend all the way over, dear. *(Washes him)* Who hit you?

YAKOV No one hit me. It's from … from a horse.

AVDOTYA From a horse?

YAKOV That's what I said—from a horse! I helped shoe a horse—and it kicked me! And don't ask me about it any more!

AVDOTYA Oh, holy mother! … You're lucky you didn't break your skull!

PYATAK It must have been a considerate horse, if it struck you so high!

YAKOV Who's that? Who said that?

AVDOTYA Only Father Kiril.

YAKOV What the hell's he doing here?

PYATAK I came to find out how the people of Israel are doing …

YAKOV Drunk, heh?

PYATAK Just tipsy …

AVDOTYA Don't turn away, darling … There. All cleaned up. Now let me bandage you.

YAKOV Where's her cotton?

TANYA Here Yashenka.

AVDOTYA It'll be fine like this. Just fine, darling. Don't worry so much. It will heal quickly.

PYATAK But there will be a scar!

TANYA Yakov, why didn't you listen to me?

YAKOV Listen to you?! … I don't give a damn about any of you! … *(To his mother)* What's she doing here? Get her out …

AVDOTYA You heard him. Out. Don't upset him …

TANYA exits.

PYATAK Why are you kicking her out? What a refined Christian soul! … Ah, Yankl, Yankl!

YAKOV You drunk pope! Say that cursed name again and I'll give you the blackest eye you've ever seen.

PYATAK Take it easy. Easy! I'm just a weakling. One blow and you'll knock me out!

YAKOV *(To his mother)* Did you hear what he called me? Yankl! He calls me Yankl!! …

AVDOTYA Did you come here just to run your mouth? Leave! There's enough going on around here without you! …

YAKOV *(To PYATAK)* I'm no Yankel, you hear? I'm an Orthodox Christian! I'd give my blood for the holy church! …

PYATAK Quietly. That's how you demonstrate your faith. With genuine kindness, just like our Savior the Lord …

YAKOV *(To his mother)* And who's to blame for this? It's all him! Why did he give me such a Jewish name? To spite me, to torment me!

AVDOTYA You have a fine name. That's how Father Timofay christened you … One of our neighbors—a cooper, I think—was named Yakov. They called him Yakov the Fool … Isn't that so, Father?

PYATAK Two of our twelve holy apostles carried the name Yakov. And Israel, the father of the twelve Jewish tribes—he was called Yakov as well …

YAKOV *(To his mother)* Hear that? A Jewish name! …

PYATAK So you're angry with your father. Why take it on your wife?

YAKOV He arranged the marriage! … Someone he would want to marry! A pale, pathetic woman everyone laughs at, and calls "The Jewess" …

PYATAK You don't deserve your wife. She has a refined soul.

YAKOV I don't need any refined souls! I wanted a healthy peasant wife. Not a dainty thing. Not someone who reads these … these Jewish books! … *(Grabs the book from the table and throws it)* Why is he dragging me into this *Zhid* stuff? Why does he give me such a hard time? … *(To his mother)* I'll get even. You'll see, you'll see …

AVDOTYA Don't talk about your father like that!

YAKOV He's not my father! …

PYATAK Your father, young man, is a rare breed. True he's stingy, like all Jews. But he's also clean, honest, straight … And sober! While we were gambling away our whole country, Moshka still has pickles in his storage-room! … Moshka—the ancient solid tree of Israel!

YAKOV But what am I? A Jew, heh? A Jew?

PYATAK No. No one will ever call you a Jew.

YAKOV Then what am I?

PYATAK You are … You are a rotten apple. Souring off that same tree.

YAKOV That so? Good. I'll show you all! …

YAKOV exits. AVDOTYA follows him out.

PYATAK (*Goes to the gilded chair*) Well. Looks like no one's going to inherit Moshka's throne! (*Sits on the chair, takes out the bottle, takes a sip*) Rotten apples!

HAVRILO enters. He is a former soldier in a ragged old soldier's uniform. He holds a broken old rifle in his hand. He has a foolish smile on his face.

HAVRILO The boss around?

PYATAK I'm the boss around here now! What do you say to that? (*HAVRILO laughs*) Why are you laughing? Spit it out!

HAVRILO It's none of your business! … I came to say that I'm exhausted. People are making trouble and the gun won't shoot anymore … (*Sees the bottle*) So you have some whiskey, Pyatak? Gimme me a swig!

PYATAK (*Hides the bottle*) Why doesn't the gun shoot?

HAVRILO The devil knows why! Hell if I do! It just won't! Even during the war this stubborn mule wouldn't budge, no matter what you did! … Gimme me a swig!

PYATAK Whiskey's not for you. Protecting Moshke's property is priority number one, so you need to be sober!

HAVRILO Just one swig … If you don't—I'll shoot! (*Points gun*)

PYATAK With my luck the gun will go off! (*Takes out the bottle*) Here, here—take a swig! But beware of God and don't gulp it all down!

HAVRILO (*Takes the bottle*) I'll just drink it like this …

HAVRILO takes a big sip, sighs with satisfaction and goes for another sip. But PYATAK takes the bottle from him.

PYATAK That's enough for you, ignorant fool! *(Puts the bottle away)* And you say there's trouble brewing? What's going on?

HAVRILO How should I know! They say he took all the kerosene, the Jewish dog! Now they're gonna make trouble. They say they're gonna do to him what they've done to all the Jews! Not even an hour ago, a peasant came from the city and said that all the Jews there had already been shot …

PYATAK Where?

HAVRILO In the city, in Muravanka. He said some had run off into the forest around here. Scared rabbits, he says …

PYATAK You barbarian! …

The door opens slowly and MOSHKE enters. He is about 50 years old, stout, hearty, his face stern, sun-burned with deep wrinkles, his hair is graying. He is dressed like a small—town burgher. Clean and neat. From his appearance and posture you wouldn't know he was Jewish. The only Jewish trait he has is the heavy look in his dark thick-browed eyes. As he enters the house, he goes straight to the table without looking at anyone and plops down in his chair. AVDOTYE grabs the bowl of water, covers it with her apron and exits momentarily. Then she returns.

MOSHKE *(To Havrilo)* What are you doing here?

HAVRILO Boss, I came to tell you …

MOSHKE Who's guarding the mill?

HAVRILO Alyoshke, my son. But the people, boss …

MOSHKE Get back to the mill! Now!

HAVRILO As you wish, master. But the gun …

MOSHKE Back to the mill, you son of a bitch!

HAVRILO exits.

PYATAK (*Quietly gets off the gilded chair and sneaks away*) You should listen to what he has to say, Ferapontov ...

MOSHKE You, too? What the hell's everybody doing here? Get out!

PYATAK I see you're very angry. I understand ... But you should hear me out.

MOSHKE Not now! Get out! Everyone out! Out of my sight, you sons of bitches! ...

PYATAK I'm going, I'm going ...!

PYATAK exits.

MOSHKE Scum! Animals! ... (*To AVDOTYE*) Where's Yakov?

AVDOTYE Yakov ...

MOSHKE Talk to me! (*TANYE enters*) Has Yakov come back?

TANYE Well ...

MOSHKE Look me in the eye. I asked you a question. Did he come back?

AVDOTYE He came back. Of course, he came back!

MOSHKE When?

TANYE Before midday. When he heard about the trouble in the city, he didn't go for the boots.

MOSHKE Ah! Where did he go then?

TANYE Where could he go? Maybe to the mill, somewhere like that ...

MOSHKE (*Notices a piece of bread that PYATAK has left on a chair. Turns to his wife*) Why's there bread lying around, huh?

AVDOTYE How did that bread get there?

MOSHKE That's what I am asking! Who's leaving bread out to spoil?

TANYE I took a piece. Please don't be angry, sir. I was hungry …

MOSHKE *(Softer)* No sin to eat. But put the leftovers away.

TANYE I must've forgot.

MOSHKE People are dying because they have no bread to eat …

TANYE takes the bread and exits. Pause.

AVDOTYE You won't get mad, Moshke?

MOSHKE Go ahead.

AVDOTYE I wanted to tell you … Our Yakov …

MOSHKE What about him?

AVDOTYE He only scratched his forehead …

MOSHKE What do you mean? How?

AVDOTYE While he was helping shoe a horse, it … kicked him.

MOSHKE Whose horse?

AVDOTYE I don't know. A village peasant asked him for help.

MOSHKE Why was he shoeing other people's horses?

AVDOTYE Don't be hard on him …

MOSHKE Where is he? Go find him! Bring him here. Now! And send in Tanye.

AVDOTYE exits. After a while TANYE enters.

TANYE You asked to see me.

MOSHKE Tell me, dear. What is this my wife is telling me about Yakov?

TANYE — About Yakov …? You mean the scratch on his …? It's nothing. You know how Yakov loves to be around horses.

MOSHKE — Other peoples' horses …

TANYE — He's a young man. He has nothing better to do.

MOSHKE — But he shouldn't be spending time with peasants. He's not a peasant—you understand?

TANYE — I'm not to blame, sir …

MOSHKE — You're his wife. Hold a little control over him …

Pause.

TANYE — You're in a mood today, aren't you?

MOSHKE — Sit down, Tanye. Please. You're the only one I talk to around here … *(TANYE sits down at the table)* I've just come from the city and … And I saw things that would make your skin crawl! You know that I have nothing to do with Jews, yes? Good. For some time now. I don't care for them and … And they once treated me very badly. I'll spare you the details. But they're still humans! God's creatures! Well—some townspeople came. Nothing but drunken hoodlums, really. They started attacking the city of hungry people, women and small children … Such chaos! My head's splitting! My head's splitting! *(Pause)* Just imagine, this happened today. On the holiest day of the year! Today is a holy, awesome day for them! …

PYATAK enters.

PYATAK — *(Calls offstage)* Come in! Come in, Rabbi. Here we are!

Following PYATAK are MEIR BER and ROKHTCHE. MEIR is thin with an ascetic face and a graying beard. He is dressed for the holiday. He is holding something in his hands under his coat. ROKHTCHE has a delicate face. Her hair is a mess. Her coat is torn. Her eyes are lost.

MOSHKE Who are they?

PYATAK They're your own kind, Moshke. The exiled of Judah. They need to hide from the enemy …

MOSHKE There's no place for them here! None! Send them away!

PYATAK Why are you doing this? These are your kin, bone of your bone and flesh of your flesh … Moses, Moses! Deliver your stranded brothers from Egypt! …

MEYER BER *(To PYATAK)* I thought you said he was a Jew?

MOSHKE I'm not a Jew! I'm a … an apostate! An apostate!

PYATAK His name is Moshke. A name from the Holy Scriptures!

MEYER BER *(To MOSHKE)* Can it be, Moshke … Moshkele?

MOSHKE Moshkele *Khazer*? You've heard of me? That's who I am! Now will you leave?

PYATAK You know each other?

MEYIR BER We come from the same town. *(To his daughter)* Come, Rokhtche. This is no place for us …

MOSHKE Wait! You're from my town?

MEYER BER *Vos iz di nafke miyne? Geven amol Shmuel Mikhl der khazen …*

MOSHKE You were the cantor? You? No … His son? And what … What's your name?

MEYIR VER *Vos iz di nafke miyne? Meyer Ber …*

MOSHKE I remember a boy by that name …

PYATAK Don't tell me you're old friends? Joseph recognized his brothers …?

MOSHKE *(Points to ROKHTCHE)* And this—who? Your …

MEYER BER *A tokhter.*

MOSHKE — A grown daughter? She can sit if she'd like. Tanye, give her a chair. She looks exhausted … *(Points to the white talis bag MEYER BER is holding)* What's that? Your money?

MEYER BER — *Gelt? Neyn, siz mayn talis.*

MOSHKE — So you were in synagogue?

MEYER BER — That's where we've come from. Tonight is *Yom Kiypper*. Our "guests" arrived at the synagogue just before *Kol Nidray* …!

YAKOV and AVDOTYE enter.

ROKHTCHE — *(Seems to recognize YAKOV and is frightened by him) Tateh, lomiyr avek fun danent! Lomiyr avek! …*

MOSHKE — Who's she afraid of?

MEYER BER — Him, apparently. *(Points to YAKOV)*

MOSHKE — Silly girl. This is my son!

Act Two

The next morning. The morning of Yom Kippur. The same set as in the first act. We hear a voice praying. Intermittently, the voice is silent and then it is heard again more quietly.

TANYE — There's no need to be afraid. No one's here. You shouldn't stay in that dark cellar all day … You speak Russian?

ROKHTCHE — Yes.

TANYE — Can I offer you some food? It's a fast day for you, I think … *(TANYE hears the praying)* I'll close the door, in case someone comes to visit. *(She exits and reenters)* Now we won't be disturbing your father's prayers … Do you need to pray?

ROKHTCHE — No.

TANYE — You don't pray?

ROKHTCHE — There's no one to pray to.

TANYE — What's your name?

ROKHTCHE — What's the difference? *(Pause)* We're only passing through. We won't be staying long …

TANYE — I know. But I feel so sorry for you.… And. Well. I thought we should talk about something pleasant …

ROKHTCHE Something pleasant? Why?

TANYE Not all people are bad.

ROKHTCHE That's makes it even more difficult …

TANYE *(Pause)* Do you mind if I ask you something? *(ROKHTCHE doesn't answer)* This is very difficult for me.… Why were you so frightened when you saw my husband?

ROKHTCHE Your husband?

TANYE The one who came in with a bandage on his head.

ROKHTCHE Oh.

TANYE Have you ever seen him before? Anywhere?

ROKHTCHE I don't remember.

TANYE Did they … harm you?

ROKHTCHE Who?

TANYE The hoodlums … Your body. It's …

ROKHTCHE You like to pry, don't you?

TANYE God forbid, why would you say that? I'm suffering too … It's no easier for me than for you!

ROKHTCHE You're so weak …

TANYE What about you?

ROKHTCHE I'm prepared to die.

TANYE You were so scared yesterday!

ROKHTCHE Yesterday feels like years ago …

TANYE You say strange things. And there's something odd about your appearance. Such a young face and already your hair's turning gray …

ROKHTCHE Gray?

TANYE You didn't know? Right here, near the temples.

ROKHTCHE *(She takes two locks of hair from both sides in her fingers)* Gray. Such a long night in the cellar … Do you have a mirror?

TANYE gets her a mirror. A pause.

TANYE Here.

ROKHTCHE I have to see it. *(Looks in the mirror)* I've gone gray. Gray … I've already come to the end of my life. My entire life …

AVDOTYE enters.

AVDOTYE I've been with the cows all morning. Just couldn't get away. Tanye, go watch for a while. I left them alone by the mill. *(TANYE does not move)* Tanike, do you hear me?

TANYE Later.

AVDODYA Why is she sitting by the window? People can see her. The cellar is good enough for them!

TANYE Enough.

AVDOTYE Who do you think you're talking to?

TANYE Shut up.

YAKOV enters, sees ROKHTCHE and becomes uncomfortable.

TANYE My God, my God.

YAKOV *(To his mother)* What's going on? What's this *khayke* doing in the house? I thought you had stuck them in the cellar!

TANYE She is holy!

AVDOTYE — Some holy person she is! She's so concerned about her appearance that she needs a mirror …

TANYE — Her hair turned gray over night!

YAKOV — *(To AVDOTYE)* If she likes them so much—she can join them in the cellar! Where she belongs!

TANYE — And you? You … You …

YAKOV — What? What does she want from me?

TANYE — These are your, your victims! You and those thugs attacked them yesterday!

YAKOV — What makes you think it was me?

TANYE — At least make an effort to deny it! Say something!

YAKOV — Why is she picking on me, mama?

AVDOTYE — Really, why? Why are making up stories about him? … He's your husband! …

TANYE exits.

YAKOV — Now she's running off to tell papa!

AVDOTYE — No, she won't. She covered for you just yesterday. Very cleverly, too! She convinced your father that you weren't in the city … She told him you came back because you sensed trouble! I wouldn't have had the brains to think that one up! You find fault with her for no reason …

YAKOV — She can go to hell! Mama, I came to get something to eat.

AVDOTYE — I didn't cook anything today.

YAKOV — You didn't cook?

AVDOTYE — He told me not to …

YAKOV — What's this all of a sudden? … Is he making us observe one of his Jewish fast days?

AVDOTYE He's the boss around here …

YAKOV That so? Not only does he hide his lepers here, but he makes us celebrate Jewish holidays as well? Mama! We have to put a stop to this!

AVDOTYE Oh how God must love you, dear …

YAKOV Why are you giving in? Why are you so faithful to him? Like a puppy! Are you a Christian? Give me a piece of bread and I'll go. You disgust me!

AVDOTYE Right away, Yashenka … *(Starts toward the door and turns around)* Listen, darling … Talking to me like that won't accomplish anything. Don't start up with him. He's your father and he's stronger than you …

YAKOV We'll see who's stronger!

AVDOTYE He's angry today. He's worried about … *(Points to Yakov's forehead)*

YAKOV Did he say something?

AVDOTYE He didn't sleep at all last night. He paced around the house, asking Tanye why you're not here over and over again!

YAKOV I could give a damn about them! Gimme a piece of bread!

AVDOTYE exits. YAKOV takes the mirror from the table and looks in it.

YAKOV What a pathetic family!

AVDOTYE enters.

AVDOTYE Here. Bread and cheese. *(YAKOV stuffs the food into his pockets, goes toward the door with AVDOTYE following him)* Listen … If he questions you, don't you dare provoke him. Tell him everything exactly as it happened. About the horse, that you weren't in the city …

YAKOV — Why are you treating me like a child? Telling me what I should say? I'll tell him! …

ALYOSHKE pokes his head in.

ALYOSHKE — You're serving food, ma'am? I'll take the cows out to pasture then …

AVDOTYE — You think I'd give you food? Get out of here before I get the poker!

ALYOSHKE goes to leave.

YAKOV — Why throw him out? Come right in, Alyoshke! Don't worry about a thing! *(To his mother)* Why are you throwing the Christians out of our house?

ALYOSHKE enters.

AVDOTYE — A Christian? He's an animal! He sucks cows' milk straight from the udder!

ALYOSHKE — May God strike me dead, ma'am! Other people do it! Everyone, ma'am … They're upset at the boss because of his kerosene. They take their anger out by sucking the milk … *(He walks around if he were looking for something)*

AVDOTYE — Who are you looking for?

ALYOSHKE — I'm looking for the Jews … They said that—you have a house full of Jews.

YAKOV — Who said?

ALYOSHKE — Akim. Said a whole group of Jews snuck through here in the middle of the night, armed with guns. A cannon, even …

YAKOV — Hear that, mama? A cannon!

AVDOTYE — He can drop dead! …

ALYOSHKE *(Laughs)* The townspeople are afraid to come near your yard.

YAKOV We don't have any Jews! We have nothing to do with Jews! We are devout Christians!

ALYOSHKE If you want … I can go into the village and tell them.

YAKOV Go and tell everyone!

ALYOSHKE *(To YAKOV secretly)* You promised me some dry cheese, sir …

YAKOV Here. *(Gives his a piece of cheese from his pocket)*

ALYOSHKE *(Looks at the cheese dissatisfied)* You promised me a whole one … If the boss were to find out, he'd give me two! *(Points out the window)* There he is!

ALYOSHKE slips out. YAKOV tries to as well, but bumps into his father.

MOSHKE There you are. I've been looking for you …

YAKOV I'm going out.

MOSHKE Later. You stay right here! *(To AVDOTYE)* And you! Go see to the cows.

AVDOTYE Tanye's taking care of them.

MOSHKE Did you hear what I just said? You're not needed here!

AVDOTYE I'm going, I'm going …

AVDOTYE exits.

MOSHKE Sit down. *(YAKOV doesn't move)* You heard me. Sit down!

YAKOV *(Sits mumbling)* Always mouthing off …

MOSHKE Don't mumble. How many times have I told you that? Did you sleep at the mill last night?

YAKOV Where else would I sleep?

MOSHKE At home! We have someone to guard the mill … Did you slip out of the house yesterday? Why?

YAKOV You let these … Jews in.

MOSHKE What's this? *(Points to the bandage)*

YAKOV Why are you asking me about every little thing? You think I'm still a child? I'm not!

MOSHKE Answer me when I talk to you!

YAKOV I got kicked by a horse.

MOSHKE Whose?

YAKOV What's the difference? It was a horse … I was passing a smith, and a peasant called me over to help him.

MOSHKE Which smith?

YAKOV The … the one from Novodvorts.

MOSHKE Things are always happening to you. Were you in Muravanka?

YAKOV Why would anyone want to be there with all this trouble brewing? I turned right around … I'll buy myself a pair of boots some other time.

MOSHKE You did the right thing.

YAKOV I know what I'm supposed to do.

MOSHKE Then listen, Yakov. I'll speak to you as an adult if you treat me with respect. Why do you always look away from me when I talk?

YAKOV Where should I look?

MOSHKE Directly at me. In the eye. Like a decent human being. Not some buffoon. You're not a peasant. How would you feel about leaving the village?

YAKOV Leaving the village?

MOSHKE Leaving here for good …

YAKOV To go where?

MOSHKE Far away from here. Change our whole lifestyle … Are you making faces? Say something!

YAKOV Do I have to go?

MOSHKE That's why we're talking about this now!

YAKOV Why should I leave the village?

MOSHKE Because I don't want you to remain a peasant. And because I'm a stranger here. This has never felt like home for me … I wasn't born among peasants. And you—you are my son. I brought you into this world. You have to follow me … And it's time.

YAKOV Do you want to return … to the Jews?

MOSHKE I don't know … We have to consider all of our options.

YAKOV And you want to drag me along?

MOSHKE I won't force you. You have to want to on your own. *(Pause)* Think it over … there's still time …

YAKOV Can I go now?

MOSHKE Remember what we talked about here. And … don't spend so much time with those good for nothings! Those fools think that I have an entire squadron of Jews with guns … Idiots. Let them think whatever they want!

YAKOV exits.

MOSHKE *(Calls offstage)* You can come in. No one will bother you. You'll be able to pray here. *(MEYER BER appears in the doorway with a prayer shawl on and holding a prayer book. His eyes take some time to adjust to the light)* Wait a minute … *(He goes to close the front door and then returns)* Pray as loud as you like. No one will disturb you. *(MEYER BER notices the icon)* What? *(MOSHKE notices the icon.)* Oh—that? The icon? I forgot! *(Climbs on a chair and takes down the icon and the holy lamp)* Don't be afraid. He doesn't hear anything. It's just a piece of wood! *(Carries them away and returns)*

MEYER BER watches MOSHKE, then goes to the eastern wall of the room and begins to rock back and forth with closed eyes holding his prayer book closed with a finger in it to mark his page. He prays quietly at first and then as it gets a little louder we recognize it as the "Olaynu." He becomes more animated as he approaches the climax "shelo som khelkeynu koyhem vi goroyleyno kikhol hamoynom." He falls to his knees singing quietly "va anachnu koyrim" and then his voice drops off into a wail as he covers his head with his prayer shawl. Then he stands up, rocks and says something from memory. He turns around and sees MOSHKE staring at him. MEYER BER stops praying, opens his prayerbook and prays silently.

MOSHKE — Care to sit down? There's more light here. *(MEYER BER comes to sit at the table with his prayer book) Gefaln koyrim*, didn't you? See? I remember some things … *(Smiles)* When the congregation bowed down for *Koyrim*, the children in the synagogue would pinch their behinds. Such rascals! *(Looks in the prayer-book)* What's this? A *siydder?* A *khumish*?

MEYER BER — It's a *makhzer*.

MOSHKE — A *makhzer*? I remember … A *makhzer*. I went to school for a while. I studied the *siydder*, the *makhzer*. But I forgot it all! I was already such a renegade by then. A Moshkele *Khazer* … Even then I didn't want to study! *(Pause)* What are you then? A cantor? A teacher?

MEYER BER — I'm neither a *khazn* nor a teacher.

MOSHKE — I had two teachers. One had black hair, and the other had blond hair. I hated them both. They tormented me. I didn't want to study, so they made my life miserable … My father was also a troublemaker when he was young. He was kicked out of his home. Well, he's long dead … Do you remember him?

MEYER BER Of course!

MOSHKE I remember your father, the cantor. Quiet man. *(Silence)* So, what do you think? Is it good to be an apostate?

MEYER BER You should know that better than I.

MOSHKE And who is to blame? All of you sons of bitches … It was all your fault. You lousy bastards! I was a kid, a wild kid. I didn't want to study, didn't want to pray. I hated the bent shoulders … The sour faces. I was a boy. I wanted to have a good time … So? Did they have to kick me out? They gave me the name "Moshkele *Khazer*." They made me join the army … Aaah, to hell with them! Moshkele *Khazer*? Well, I'll show you who Moshkele *Khazer* is!

MEYER BER You already showed me …

MOSHKE You are the swine! Bigger pigs than I am! *(Points to his heart)* What happened in here, no one knows … It's been twenty-five years. Twenty-five years. I've been a convert. With peasants. With imbeciles. I was … I was …

MEYER BER *(Pause)* If that's the way it is … you can still change your mind. Everyone is free now. Now you can be the target of a pogrom just like everyone else …

MOSHKE I'm not afraid of a pogrom. There are worse things. But where could I go? Back to the *shtetl*? They'll only mock me. Isn't that Moshkele *Khazer*? Has Moshkele *Khazer* returned home with his whip? … I hate your *shtetl Zhids.* They're all a bunch of nobodies. Parasites and swindlers! …

MEYER BER You really do talk like an apostate …

MOSHKE I speak the truth! *(Silence)* Where would I go?

MEYER BER Where?

MOSHKE *(Gets a newspaper from his bookcase)* Can you read Russian?

MEYER BER Yes.

MOSHKE *(Turns to a specific page and shows him)* What does it say here? Under the picture?

MEYER BER What are you doing with this?

MOSHKE Read, read!

MEYER BER *(He reads)* "Jewish farmers in Palestine …"

MOSHKE There! That's where I'd like to go! They say the British are going to give it to you. Is that true?

MEYER BER So they say … How do you know?

MOSHKE I know everything! What do you think, Moshkele *Khazer* is a boor? Illiterate? … See these books? All these newspapers? I bought them all! I didn't just find them! At forty I learned to read—I taught myself! *(Points to the article in the newspaper.)* That's where I'd go! To plow. To plant and mill. Like other people—not like you with your bad posture. Good machines there. I'd buy a farm, work, keep to myself. I'd have nothing to do with anyone.

MEYER BER Maybe it's not such a bad idea …

MOSHKE So you agree? What do I have to do?

MEYER BER Do?

MOSHKE I'm asking … Is there something I have to do?

MEYER BER To become a Jew again?

MOSHKE Yes!

MEYER BER What is there to do? You're a Jew—and that's it.

MOSHKE That simple?

MEYER BER What do I know? Go ask a rabbi if you want to …

MOSHKE — No—I hate priests, I hate rabbis. Why go to a rabbi? He'll just criticize me …

MEYER BER — On the contrary!

MOSHKE — What would he do?

MEYER BER — Probably tell you to accept upon yourself a penitence.

MOSHKE — Accept what?

MEYER BER — Penitence. To repent.

MOSHKE — Like what?

MEYER BER — Lord only knows. Fast, possibly …

MOSHKE — Fast? That's nothing! I can do that easily … What else?

MEYER BER — Give charity, perhaps …

MOSHKE — Give charity? To whom?

MEYER BER — To the poor.

MOSHKE — The poor? Why do those parasites deserve charity? Let them work! Dig the ground! Chop wood! Then they'll have some charity!

MEYER BER — What about sick people and orphans?

MOSHKE — Sick people are different. That's a shame … For sure. There's nothing else I have to do?

MEYER BER — You were born to Jewish parents … According to Jewish law, you've been a Jew all along. *Yisroyl, af al piy shekhoto, Yisroyl hu Yisroel, af al piy shekhoto, Yisroyl hu.*

MOSHKE — What's that?

MEYER BER — A Jew, whatever he may do, still remains a Jew … That's what the Talmud says.

MOSHKE — That Talmud is one smart book! They got it just right!

MEYER BER — You can even be included in a *minyen.*

MOSHKE — In a what?

MEYER BER A *minyen.* When nine Jews need a tenth to pray, you can be that tenth!

MOSHKE I never knew! But pray—I can't do that. I forgot how! So many years have gone by. I was a fool, such a fool …

MEYER BER What about your wife?

MOSHKE A wife is like a calf. Tie her up with a rope and she'll follow you … For twenty-five years I've been a *goy* for her. Enough! Now she can do whatever she wants. If she wants to she can come, if she doesn't she can stay here. There's a son in the picture. That presents a problem …

MEYER BER What does he do?

MOSHKE Nothing! And, and … another thing! We also have a daughter-in-law, an educated young woman. But what good is a daughter-in-law if your son is a devil? It's not easy to become an apostate, it's not easy to be a Jew … *(There is a knock at the front door. Moshke peers out the window)* Who's there?

AVDOTYE *(From offstage)* Open up, Moshke!

MOSHKE What's going on? I told you you're not needed here!

PYATAK Let me in, sir! It's important!

MOSHKE goes to the door and opens it. He comes back followed by AVDOTYE, PYATAK and TANYE.

AVDOTYE You weren't expecting this, Moshke!

TANYE What a disaster! An absolute disaster! …

PYATAK It's not happy news, Moshke. *(To MEYER BER)* God help us, Mister Rabbi!

MOSHKE What happened?

PYATAK People are on their way!

TANYE They're coming from the woods. Alyoshke told …

AVDOTYE And there you have it, Moshke!

MOSHKE Why are they coming here?

PYATAK They found out that there are only two of them here …

MOSHKE Who told them?

PYATAK A little bird …

MOSHKE What bird? Maybe you were the bird!

PYATAK Moshke, you insult me! May God forgive you! …

MOSHKE Who told them then?

TANYE Now is not the time! We have to do something!

AVDOTYE They should go! Get out of here! The mob will destroy our house!

MEYER BER Where is my daughter? We're leaving …

MOSHKE No, she'll leave before you do! *(To AVDOTYE)* Shut up, you … You … butcher's daughter! … *(To MEYER BER)* You'll have to go back into the cellar.

MEYER BER Not back there. I want to be with my daughter …

TANYE I'll go to your daughter, sir … Let me go to her! It'll be better this way. I won't let them touch her …

TANYE exits.

MOSHKE Where is Havrilo? (*To PYATAK)* Lock the door behind me. Don't let anyone in! And he must stay here, he must not leave!

MOSHKE exits. PYATAK locks the door after him.

AVDOTYE God is punishing us!

PYATAK Please. Don't frighten us more than we already are …

AVDOTYE And since when do you tell me what to do?

PYATAK You'd better go keep an eye on the bird …

AVDOTYE What bird?

PYATAK Your bird, actually. I hope the old man doesn't find him.

AVDOTYE You're right, Father! Oh, what a disaster!

AVDOTYE exits.

PYATAK *(Follows her out to lock the door behind her and then comes back and says under his breath)* A bird of prey! … *(To MEYER BER)* Be strong, Mister Rabbi. Be strong! I'm with you … I—a former spiritual figure! Your holiday clothes are magnificent! You only see such clothing in holy paintings … What do they call you, holy man? Elijah?

MEYER BER Excuse me?

PYATAK What is your name?

MEYER BER Meyer Ber.

PYATAK Sit down, Mister Meyer Ber. You'll feel alot better if you sit … *(MEYER BER obeys him mechanically. PYATAK sits opposite him)* Meyer Ber … What a wonderful sounding name. A musician's name! Mendelssohn, Rubinstein, Meyer Ber—all are Jews. And I, dear sir, cannot pride myself with my name. It's such a measly name. It's my honor to introduce myself—Pyatak! *(Bows and sits down again)* A puny name. All in all, only ten groshn … of the old currency! It now must be worth a million, but it's still not enough to buy a shot of good whiskey … What a time we live in! *(Pause)* What do you think? You Jews will actually take over the world? I think so. The fact that everyone is against you makes you superior to everyone else. Suffering, dear man, elevates a person … *(Pause)* Meyer Ber … I once read about him in a book. When I was young and sang in the municipal church, I was drawn to the great composers. I almost became a performer, if you can believe it! I felt, dear sir, that I had so many talents. But what became of all of it in the end? *(Takes out his bottle and takes a sip)* Here. Fortify yourself … *(Puts the bottle in front of him)* Jesus, our Lord, your blood brother, also drank wine during the Last Supper. Before they came to take him away … *(MEYER BER tries to reach the door but PYATAK blocks his way)* Where are you going?

MEYER BER Let me go! Let me out! …

PYATAK Where do you want to go, you're out of your mind? … *(MEYER BER tears himself away)* Here comes Moshke!

MOSHKE enters followed by HAVRILO, who is carrying his gun.

HAVRILO Where should I stand—right here?

MOSHKE Not here—outside! By the door. Don't let anyone in!

HAVRILO Anything you say, boss! *(Points his gun at the Jew)* Is that him?

MOSHKE Go. This isn't your business!

HAVRILO Anything you say, boss. What should I tell them?

MOSHKE Say: "I was ordered not to let you in!"

HAVRILO And if they start forcing their way in?

MOSHKE Chase them away! Shoot! Shoot in the air!

HAVRILO It's easy for you to say "shoot," boss … This nasty thing doesn't always fire.

MOSHKE Just go!

HAVRILO Anything you say boss. It's not worth making such a fuss over one *Zhiyd.*

MOSHKE Idiot! *(To MEYER BER)* You should really go into the cellar! So they don't see you.…

HAVRILO enters.

HAVRILO Boss! They're already here! …

MOSHKE Huh? *(We hear voices)* To the door! The door, imbecile! Barricade the door!

HAVRILO exits. MOSHKE grabs MEYER BER who has wandered over to the window.

MOSHKE And you! Why are you standing where they can see you?

MOSHKE pushes MEYER BER into another room and grabs an ax.

PYATAK As God is my witness! You'll only provoke them …

PYATAK takes the ax from MOSHKE and puts it back in its place. The noise in the yard grows. A hoard of peasants approaches the window, men and women, pushing each other. You can now make out what they are saying: "Is he here?" "Yes, he's here!" "Aha, now we'll finally get him!" "What a tight-wad!" "Three barrels of kerosene hidden!" "What kerosene? He's hiding the Jews!" "A Jew remains a Jew!" "Cursed antichrist!" "They bring every disaster!" "The people are hungry." "They shot all the priests!" "What, just priests? They tortured the tsar!" "They didn't, the commissars did!" "Don't pick on him!" "Don't pick on Christians!" "Here come people who are smarter than you—move aside!" "Let us through!" Then the voices go suddenly silent. The door opens and four peasants appear. LEADER has a small gun. The other three have axes in their belts. Behind these four, AKIM slips in. LEADER pushes away the crowd outside and closes the door.

LEADER Who here is called "Ferapontov"?

MOSHKE I am Ferapontov!

LEADER — Are you a Christian? *(MOSHKE does not answer. LEADER raises his voice and repeats)* A Christian?

PYATAK — Of course he's a Christian, sir. And what a Christian he is! Baptized and all!

LEADER — *(To PYATAK)* And who are you?

PYATAK — God's servant, sir. It's my honor. Kiril Kirilich … *(Bows)*

LEADER — And what kind of hat would you call that?

PYATAK — *(Takes off his hat)* The last hat that's left in holy Russia.

LEADER — *(To AKIM)* Who is this? He's a suspicious character!

AKIM — He's one of ours. He once served in our church. He's got a screw loose …

PYATAK — With you around, fine man, I feel as safe as in Christ's bosom.

LEADER — *(To MOSHKE)* Where are the Jews?

MOSHKE — Jews? What Jews?

LEADER — You've been hiding two Jews. A father and daughter.

MOSHKE — Hoodlum! Who d'you think you are? *(To the TOWNSPEOPLE)* You good-for-nothings! How dare you enter my house without permission? Why are you still standing here? Hats off, imbeciles! *(The TOWNSPEOPLE remove their hats)*

LEADER — *(To the TOWNSPEOPLE)* I see that you consider him a governor-general! Put your hats back on! *(The TOWNSPEOPLE obey him)*

AKIM — He is a tough one …

MOSHKE — You, Akim! You should be ashamed of yourself. Sly fox! Haven't I done enough favors for you? Why're you here?

AKIM — Me? Just tagging along. I'm here only out of curiosity …

MOSHKE I'll show you some curiosity!

LEADER Enough! Hand over the Jews!

MOSHKE I don't have any Jews! And I won't allow you to behave so despicably here! I'm one of the most prominent members of this village!

LEADER We'll soon see ... *(Goes to search the house)*

MOSHKE Don't take another step!

LEADER You're not going to let us?

MOSHKE You can't go in there!

PYATAK *(To LEADER)* Sir—in the name of Christianity! Don't go in there! Don't go into hell!

LEADER Why are you standing like a bunch of stiffs? Take him! *(The TOWNSPEOPLE bring MEYER BER from the other room)*

PYATAK God in heaven! Protect us! Have mercy!

LEADER *(To MOSHKE)* So? No Jews here, hey?

PYATAK He's not a Jew! He's holy! Look at him! Holy!

LEADER We've seen enough of these holy ones! You, old man—you sold your soul to our enemies, hey? We should give you a real whipping! *(To the TOWNSPEOPLE)* Take him away! *(Two TOWNSPEOPLE take the Jew by the arms)* Wait! The daughter's here somewhere ...

One of the other TOWNSPEOPLE looks around. MOSHKE grabs the ax.

MOSHKE Let him go! I'm warning you!

MEYER BER You don't have to. Let them ...

MOSHKE puts down the ax. LEADER takes it from him and gives it to one of the townspeople.. The door opens and the third TOWNSPERSON forces his way through with ROKHTCHE. TANYE follows them.

FARMER We found this one in the closet!

LEADER Take them both! March!

MOSHKE Stop! Wait! Wait! *(To LEADER)* How much do you want for them?

LEADER Pay? You're going to pay anyway! There's a whole crowd waiting for us!

AKIM *(To LEADER)* Commander, let me say a few words. I think that … a payment is a payment! First, let him give up the kerosene that he's stored at his mill. And his three dairy cows. And his gold watches that are buried in his stable, as everyone knows … A payment is a payment!

MOSHKE Eh, you …! …

AKIM I'm speaking to the point. How many times have I told you, Ferapontov. Don't start up with the people! But you didn't listen! Well, it serves you right …

MOSHKE Dogs! Animals! Serves me right? For twenty-five years I've lived here with you ignorant thugs. Lousy, mangy dogs! Suffocating! Smelling your stench! Choking in your filth—and this is how you treat me? Now you drag my guests from my house! Innocent, blameless people. You aren't even worthy enough to wash their feet! Take me too! Dispose of me!

LEADER Take him too then! Why are you just staring?

VOICES *(From offstage)* Take him, take him, the converted dog!

AKIM No, don't touch him! He has a Christian wife, son, and daughter-in-law. We'll deal with him ourselves, like old neighbors … *(Pulls MOSKHE aside and speaks to him quietly)* Back, Ferapontov. You're making a mistake.

MOSHKE is exhausted. He sits down on the first chair.

LEADER Let's go!

PYATAK No, I won't let this happen! We won't let this happen! We are Christians!

PYATAK gets down on his knees. TANYE does the same. They both clasp their hands in supplication.

VOICES *(From offstage)* Take him away! Pyatachok, get out of here!

PYATAK Brother Christians! What are you doing? Have mercy! Have mercy! Look, I'll beat myself for you! (Bangs his forehead against the ground) Look—I stand before you with bitter tears! Brother Christians, I want you to swear by this holy cross … *(Pulls off his shirt and searches with trembling fingers)* It's not here! The cross isn't here! I drank it away!

The TOWNSPEOPLE laugh, carry him offstage. They march out the two Jews.

PYATAK Moshke! Get the icon! Let's go out to the people with the icon! Where is the icon? Where's the icon, Moshke?!

Act Three

Same day, evening. Same set as in the first two acts. MOSHKE is sitting at the table looking in the open prayer book left by the Jew. In the last few hours he has become old. AVDOTYE enters talking to herself.

AVDOTYE — That hunchback devil's nowhere to be found. Not him, not the cows. All gone … Oh, Father in Heaven! This day is finally over … Oh, the sins we've committed! Moshke, should I make you something to eat? You haven't had any food since yesterday morning. You must be starving. Moshke! *(Pause)* What are you grieving for? He's not your brother. He's nothing to you … I remember you chased them away from here, like evil spirits. You even had me chase them away … Do you think it's been easy for me? It hasn't! *(Pause)* I've lived a lifetime with you, I gave you everything you wanted. I even sinned before God for you! Like a loyal dog! Protecting you from everything … And now? Now I have no place in your house. Earlier today you scolded me in front of strangers. You called me a "butcher's daughter". You insulted my late father. Why do I deserve this? I roam around here like a stranger. Both of us. Me and my son!

MOSHKE — Get out of here …

AVDOTYE — You're not well! Get in bed until the fever passes!

MOSHKE — Get out of my sight …

AVDOTYE exits. Short pause. Then the door opens slowly and PYATAK enters.

PYATAK — You survived, Moshke? Because I died, literally died! I'm exhausted! No strength left! *(TANYE comes out of the other room, crying)* You're still here, child?

TANYE — *(To PYATAK)* Well?

PYATAK — Don't ask, child. The pagans tortured him. Crucified him!

TANYE — Holy mother! Where did this happen?

PYATAK — On the Golgotha. On the hill near the forest …

TANYE — Both of them?

PYATAK — Both and ten others. Twelve holy martyrs, they say. Exactly twelve …

TANYE — How awful! Were you there?

PYATAK — No, child … How could I be? My legs were too weak to support me. I hid in a corner and I … fell asleep. Now I wait for a miracle. We need a miracle now! Moshke! We're living in extraordinary times! History is repeating itself right before our eyes. Not long ago I passed here, thinking: Nineteen hundred years ago this was also happening … On the streets of the holy city of Jerusalem, a small man, a homeless Kiril Kirilitch, wandered around. And while they crucified Jesus, our Lord, up there, the foundations of the world shaking—he lay below, in a ditch, drunk. He slept sweetly. I know, Moshke. You're grieving deeply. If I could, I'd grieve with you. But I'm not good at it … How can I feel sorrow when I am sorrow itself? A dry autumn leaf driven by the wind? You—you are different. You are a deeply rooted tree! You are all like old oak trees. When a storm-wind sweeps over your head, you howl to the heavens: Hoo-oo-oo-oo! And how gloriously you die! I'll die behind a fence somewhere with an empty flask in my pocket. I will shrivel up like a worm and that's it … And you! They're going to lead you to your death as if it were your wedding. Parading you! Honoring you! An entire village of pagans will follow behind you and shout: Judah's been captured! Judah's been captured! Why you had to convert, Moshke, I cannot understand … What did you think we had, exactly? What did you exchange your divine origin for? Go back! The British are calling you to return to your hold land—so go! It's a shame you brought this child into your home … What did you have against her? Such a delicate Christian soul. An orphan! Oh, the blazing sun is setting! O, Jehovah's wrath burns! They slaughtered his children! Now there's no one to sing to him on this sacred evening.

MOSHKE exits. PYATAK follows him to the door.

PYATAK What's wrong? Where are you going? He's gone mad!

AVDOTYE enters.

AVDOTYE Did he leave?

PYATAK He's gone!

AVDOTYE Where?

PYATAK I don't know. I must've said something that upset him …

AVDOTYE You old geezer! You're lucky I don't have any boiling water to pour over you!

PYATAK Why, dear woman? Why?

AVDOTYE Why, he asks! What were you blabbering about? Why are you encouraging him to go back there? Back to what? Don't I have enough trouble without you coming here and stirring things up? Why do you have to spout nonsense all the time? Jabbering away!

PYATAK Maybe you're right … But you don't have to get angry.

AVDOTYE I suppose I should thank you! I hope the devil takes you! I hope wolves eat your flesh, you black crow! Vile thing!

PYATAK Don't mention the devil, woman! One whistle will bring him flying! And the holy icon is missing. See?

AVDOTYE Holy mother! Where is it?

PYATAK Gone. Maybe because of your foul mouth! You be careful, my dear. You can still do damage. Go sit down, calm yourself. You'll be safer if you keep quiet. In silence you can feel God! *(Pause)* He left his holy Torah. I'm having a hard time making sense of this … Maybe it's the other way around? *(Turns over the prayer book)* No. This is even worse! *(To TANYE)* When I was young, in the seminary, I studied Old Hebrew script. By my second year they threw me out … For free-thinking! A shame!

TANYE *(To PYATAK)* Where could my father-in-law have gone?

PYATAK He left! The ghost of his fallen brother is chasing him.

The sun goes down and the room becomes illuminated with the light of an autumn dusk.

TANYE I feel as if I'm going mad, Father! I see her everywhere I look. I still think that someone in our family is responsible for what happened …

PYATAK We all are guilty. They died for our sins …

TANYE She's still standing in front of me … I want to sleep, but I can't! Just a while ago, I was lying down—and she came out on her tiptoes! She stood in the doorway and looked at me strangely, with such a sad smile …

PYATAK It's the same for me, child. I see him, sitting here at the table. He's wrapped in that holy garment—and there! There's a halo glowing above his head …

TANYE I followed her into the closet, it was so dark. I'll never forget! I tried to console her. I hugged her. She had such delicate shoulders, like a bird. And yet she was so strong! The whole time, she was silent. So stoic. So proud …

PYATAK He was too … He sat here deep in thought. I blabber on and he says nothing. So I ask: What do they call you, holy father? And he quietly replies: Mendelssohn. It still rings in my ears, like divine music … Mendelssohn!

TANYE She was so dignified when she gave herself up to them! She said: I'll go on my own, you don't have to carry me off! Father! Why do the books say they are cowards, that they're afraid to die?

PYATAK Because they cling tightly to life. Because they are the only ones who comprehend the deep meaning of life … They were the first and want to be the last on the earth.

TANYE And yet—they both went to their deaths so calmly!

PYATAK Not calmly, child. They'd become appalled by life …

TANYE Her hair turned gray over night. This morning, that sweet girl sat at the table staring into the mirror and repeating to herself: I've gone gray, I've gone gray! Father, I wanted to go gray too! Look—have I gone gray?

PYATAK Not yet, my dear … Only those who keep everything inside grow gray prematurely. And also those who get drunk … But you, my child, you wear your heart on your sleeve. You cry at the drop of a hat. You're weak, dear.

TANYE She said the same thing: You're so weak …

ALYOSHKE enters.

ALYOSHKE — Ma'am, ma'am! Are you here?

AVDOTYE enters.

AVDOTYE — Huh? Who's here? The hunchback?

ALYOSHKE — I came to tell you something, ma'am, …

AVDOTYE — Where did you disappear to?

ALYOSHKE — I didn't disappear—here I am! Others, ma'am, have disappeared …

AVDOTYE — What are you yacking about? What others? Yakov?

ALYOSHKE — No, not Yakov—the cows!

AVDOTYE — What about the cows? Where are the cows?

ALYOSHKE — I'm telling you—they've disappeared!

AVDOTYE — Why are you making jokes about that, you cripple?

ALYOSHKE — May God strike me down, if I'm joking! There are no more cows! Say goodbye! Akim took them!

AVDOTYE — Akim?

ALYOSHKE — The one and only! He came to the pasture with a whole gang of boys and drove them right off to his stable …

AVDOTYE — What's he going to do with my cows?

ALYOSHKE — He'll milk 'em, ma'am. Milk 'em! He says the cows belong to him, legally. Today, he says, he saved the master from certain death. If not for him, he says, the master would now be a goner!

AVDOTYE — My cows! My livelihood! *(To PYATAK)* Father, what is this? Robbery!

PYATAK — Not robbery … Requisition. That's what they call it!

AVDOTYE — I'm going after that thief right now!… *(Bumps into HAVRILO as she exits)*

HAVRILO I've had it.

AVDOTYE What's wrong?

HAVRILO I guarded, I guarded, guarded, guarded, I watched. Careful-careful, careful-careful. All for nothing!

AVDOTYE God all-merciful! Speak coherently, you fool!

HAVRILO He just barged into the mill with the whole village …

AVDOTYE The thief? Akim?

HAVRILO What Akim? Not Akim—your young master!

AVDOTYE … Yakov?

HAVRILO Dragged out the kerosene barrels, opened the sacks of bread. Here, he says, take some, Christian people!

AVDOTYE My son!

HAVRILO Here, he says. Take it, Christian people! Well, they made off with everything. Started digging up the ground, looking for wristwatches. Slugged me in the mouth! Broke the gun …

PYATAK Did you see the master?

HAVRILO You bet I did!

PYATAK Where is he?

HAVRILO He just got there.

PYATAK Well … What did he say?

HAVRILO What do you expect him to say? He just stood there!

PYATAK Just stood there?

HAVRILO He stood there watching …

PYATAK That's not like Moshke at all!

TANYE *(To AVDOTYE)* Let's get over there! Something awful is about to happen!

AVDOTYE You've got to help us save our livelihood!

TANYE and AVDOTYE exit, followed by PYATAK.

HAVRILO Why'd they break my gun? It was just a gun, after all …

ALYOSHKE Papa …

HAVRILO What?

ALYOSHKE Papa … Let's take something.

HAVRILO What do mean "take"?

ALYOSHKE Soon they'll be coming here too. They'll take everything. Let's beat them to it …

HAVRILO *(Laughs)* You're a sly one, Alyoshke! You want to steal?

ALYOSHKE Not steal. Just take some things … We have priority. We worked for this mongrel convert for next to nothing!

HAVRILO You are a sly one!

ALYOSHKE There's no one here!

HAVRILO What do you want to take?

ALYOSHKE He has a lot of dry cheese in the cabinet, jars of butter, and a silver spoon that he bought from the Count …

HAVRILO So you want to take off with it? I've heard he has it stashed away under lock and key!

ALYOSHKE So we'll break the lock!

HAVRILO I'm afraid to break it …

ALYOSHKE There are pots hanging here! Copper pots!

HAVRILO Maybe a few pots! No. They're too valuable …

ALYOSHKE They don't call you fool for nothing! Hide these under your cloths.

HAVRILO No! He'll get angry! *(Climbs up to shelf and puts the pots back)*

ALYOSHKE Such an ass! And you call yourself my father!

HAVRILO — I'm an honest soldier! I guarded the mill for him loyally! And who does a crippled hunchback serve, you son of a bitch?! Come on!

HAVRILO drags him out. For a moment the stage is empty. The light gets deeper and deeper red. MOSHKE, YAKOV and TANYE run by the window. The door opens and MOSHKE is leading YAKOV by the hand. TANYE stands in the doorway. MOSHKE pushses YAKOV into a chair.

MOSHKE — I've brought him back home! Back to his father's house!

TANYE — What are you going to do?

MOSHKE — You—you're not one of us. Leave! Only we must be here. Father and son. The father and the son …

TANYE — Moshke, don't do anything to him! Let me! I will! I am no longer weak! Yakov—pleased with yourself? Are you pleased with what you've done? What were you thinking, you animal? Get on you knees! On your knees, facing your father! On your knees! Oh, dear Yakov! Show me some kindness! At least once in your life show me some kindness! *(Gets down on her knees and hugs his legs)* Be good, Yashenko. Apologize to your father! Let's both apologize, promise that things will be different! …

YAKOV — She's glued to me. Get out of here, you … *Zhiyd!*

MOSHKE — You heard what he said? Get out … You foolish *Zhiyd*!

TANYE exits. MOSHKE locks the door behind her.

YAKOV — Why are you locking me in? Let me out! Let me out!

MOSHKE — Who are you? She's a *Zhiyd*. What does that make you?

YAKOV — A Christian!

MOSHKE — And what am I? Who brought you into the world?

YAKOV — That's not my concern … Leave me alone!

MOSHKE Whose inheritance did you give away?

YAKOV You've sucked the people's blood … Your *Zhiyds* destroyed our country! You must pay!

MOSHKE That so? Who told you that? Akim? You smell of whiskey, peasant! Guess you drank to work up the courage, huh?

YAKOV What do you want from me? Let me out! You're only making it worse! The whole village is on my side!

MOSHKE The whole village on your side! Earlier today I thought differently. I thought you'd still become something.

YAKOV Become something? What? A *Zhiyd*? *(Laughs)*

MOSHKE A human being! I wanted you to become a decent human being! Not some pig that plays in mud! Not a mad dog—a decent human being! I wanted to teach you to be kind, to be honest …

YAKOV Who are you to me? Not a father! You're my enemy! My blood enemy! You took our faith! You christened me in our church—and gave me a Jewish name! Raised me in the village—and didn't let me hang around with the other children! You were always rebuking me, always beating me! You made my life hell! You all made my life hell! From childhood—*Zhiyd, Zhiyd*! The village kids always harassed me, laughed at me! Made me strip naked and stared … Now I'm paying you back for everything. For everything … Why didn't you drop dead there, among your *Zhiyds*, before you came here to us?!

MOSHKE Enough, little peasant … Tell me now! It was you who sent the gang here today!

YAKOV And if I did—so what?

MOSHKE And you were in Moravanka yesterday too?

YAKOV So what?

MOSHKE And you were raising hell with all the animals? You beat up Jews, huh? Beat Jews? And you got this when a horse kicked you?

MOSHKE pulls off his bandage. We see a scar from which blood is still dripping. YAKOV puts his hand over his forehead. MOSHKE pulls YAKOV's hand away.

MOSHKE A red mark ... A bloody mark! Who did this? The Jews? They made a sign? Moshkele *Khazer*'s son? No, not a human! He! He did it! God! Like He did to him, that man in the holy book! The Jewish book ... Now I understand! Now I understand! And you want to go on living with this? Walk this earth? No! I must uproot it! Uproot it with my own hands! *(Grabs YAKOV)* Come!

YAKOV Let me go! Papa! Let me go! Let go! Where are you taking me?

MOSHKE Into the cellar! Where the Jews were! Uproot, uproot with my own hands! *(Drags YAKOV offstage)*

YAKOV *(From offstage)* Papa, let go! You're making it worse!

We hear a body fall and the rattling of keys. MOSHKE re-enters.

MOSHKE Like this, my son! I will uproot—uproot from the divine origin! *(We hear banging)* Banging, my son? You'll soon stop. Where's the kerosene? You gave it away to the Christians, but there must be some left. Where is it? There! *(Drags the bottle of kerosene from a corner)* There's a bit left. It's enough for both. For the father and the son. *(Goes to the door, pouring from the bottle as he walks)* For father and son. *(In a while we see flames)* Uproot. Uproot our divine origins! *(Paces and then suddenly stops, as if he sees someone)* You may sit there. No one will disturb you. *(Approaches the table mischeiveously. Grabs the prayer book and hides it under his shirt)* I have the right, I have the right, I am entitled! *(We see flames and thick smoke)*

CURTAIN

978-0-595-47142-3
0-595-47142-0